MOUNTAIN
FOOTFALLS

Biography

The present work is Ian Mitchell's fifth mountaineering book. The first, with Dave Brown, was *Mountain Days and Bothy Nights*, which has become a classic of mountain writing. This was followed by *A View from the Ridge*, also co-authored with Dave Brown, which won the Boardman-Tasker Prize for Mountain Literature in 1991. Ian has further collaborated on a biography of A.E. Robertson, *The First Munroist*, with Pete Drummond.

From his solo pen has come *Second Man on the Rope* (also published by Mercat Press), an account of his travels and climbs with Dave Brown (described by *Scotland on Sunday* as 'Jim Kelman meets Chris Bonington'). Ian also writes regularly for the outdoor press on the Scottish mountain scene, and on his travels further afield in the Pyrenees, the Alps, Norway and Iceland. He is currently working on a book on the pre-history of mountaineering in Scotland, *The Mountains before the Mountaineers*.

MOUNTAIN FOOTFALLS
A Calendar of the Scottish Hills

IAN MITCHELL

**MERCAT
PRESS**

First published in 1996 by Mercat Press
James Thin, 53 South Bridge, Edinburgh EH1 1YS

Typeset in Palatino 10/12 point at Mercat Press
Printed by Athenaeum Press Ltd

Dedication

This work is dedicated to the Bash Street Kids. And to the memories of Hamish Dhu, Coinneach an Airidh, Maggie, Bob and all the others—but most of all to that of Murdo MacDonald of Crola, Lewis.

Acknowledgements

Some of the materials which form the basis of the present work have previously appeared in the following publications: *The Great Outdoors*, *High*, *Countryman*, the *Press and Journal*, the *West Highland Free Press*, and the *Herald*.

Contents

Introduction:
THE ECHO CHAMBER

A mountaineering publisher once advised me that if I had found a successful formula I should stick to it. Possibly the fact that he refused, in succession, three of my books later published elsewhere, led me to doubt the wisdom of his advice. I would hope that none of my books, the present work included, could be guilty of the charge of being written to a formula, though I leave judgement to the reader.

I would like to think that *Mountain Footfalls* carries on from my previous mountain writing, and also brings new angles to bear. On the one hand readers familiar with previous works will find here mountain tales, often bothy-focused, concerning the great middle ground of mountain experience. In these—as in previous tales—I have tried to point out, especially to novices, that there is a great tradition of Scottish mountaineering, whose footfalls you are echoing. The climbs, the paths, the howffs, did not appear yesterday. They have a history, which should be appreciated.

But the more I walk the hills, the more I become aware that I am hearing echoes which resonate with other echoes, footfalls on footfalls. The history of the pre-clearance Highlands is known to us largely through myth and legend, few of its marks remaining visible on the landscape we pass through. Yet the culture and social structure which replaced it has only recently undergone its death-agony over much of Scotland. The early mountaineers—and even those of the post World War II generation—were in a unique position to witness that culture, inter-relate with it and record it. Alas, how few of the mountaineers I meet listen for these footfalls.

Before you, reader, came other mountaineers whose doings are worthy of remembrance, and of becoming familiar with. But before them there were others: people who were there not for leisure, but for work. They did not have the choices you do, but they loved the land you walk in, though maybe in a different way, and they shaped the scenery you see with your eyes. They have a right to your respect and to your remembrance. And just as the history of mountaineering has as much, if not more, to do with the broad masses of the middle ground, rather than with the superstars, so too should the history of our bens and glens have more to do with its ordinary inhabitants—another great middle ground—than with the mythologies of Prince Charlie or the clan chiefs. Thus this work departs from my previous ones by delving into the history of the people who came before, and later coexisted with, the mountaineers.

When you make your footfalls on the mountains, you are not exercising as in a running track or a gym. Nor are you simply experiencing beauty, as in a museum or gallery. With your eyes and ears you can see and hear what has gone before you, appropriate it and immeasurably enrich your experience. With the hope that it might help you in that direction, I give you this book.

January:
IMMORTAL MEMORY

A hard rain. The drops battering the window faster than the wipers could clear them. Kaleidoscopic light effects of oncoming car beams, then darkness with the hills invisible as the Moor was crossed, with the Lad at the wheel. Scotland. January. Rain, cold, darkness. Rain, wind, darkness. There was not much to say, and we had said it. So we passed silently through the Fort, heading for Glenfinnan.

The Young Pretender was invisible on his tower behind us, as was MacAlpine's concrete viaduct before us, and we sat waiting, watching the rain—for nothing else was visible, though the wind made itself heard above the drumming of drops on the roof. The others had not yet arrived, so we were waiting. I felt the need to say something, to break the black spell the rain was casting.

'It's like,' I ventured, 'Yon bit in one o Marquez's novels, where it rains and rains. They all watch it, and eventually ging mad, as hooses collapse and the graves gie forth their deid...'

'But it least it was warm there. It's freezing here. Let's go tae the pub and wait for the rest o them,' was the reply.

Winter in the Highlands is like one long, miserable Presbyterian Sunday: everything is shut. So, after ferreting about down wee lanes and finding every hotel around closed up, the Lad opted to drive back to the Fort—all of fifteen miles for a pint. We were there in fifteen minutes.

It took us a while to find it, in a rickle of outbuildings round the back of a very closed hotel, but we followed the lights and crossed the threshold. Instantly I felt we had made a mistake, and wondered whether we should be there at all. Not that it was a barn of a place, with all the charm of a Portakabin. Not that—although it had to be admitted it didn't rain nor the wind blow inside—it was at least as cold as it was outside. Not that the barmaids were a pair of Amazons who looked like female mud wrestlers on their day off. Not that the denizens of the pub were that mongrel crew of the Fort's housing estates—second generation Glesca keelies now on the dole with the

1

pulp mill closed, and semi-urbanised tinker-types, who gave the High Noon eye when we walked in the door. Rather it was the uneasy feeling that this place might not have an official right to be open, and that those there might feel we were checking up on it. We were gulping our way through our pints when the barmaid came over, to be friendly. As she spoke, darts were poised in mid-throw, cues stilled mid-stroke. And lugs were cocked.

'Hello, boys, where ye off to on a night like this?' Now the Lad is charm itself, a walking encyclopaedia of social skills—and a good-looking fella forbye. So he soon had the Amazon relaxed and eating out of his hand, and virtually sitting on his lap, offering to refill our glasses. I saw problems. The Amazons might be won over, but we were still getting O.K. Corral looks from the guys. Never mess with the local women—if there are local lads around—is my motto. So I managed to extract him from the charming hostelry, as verbal equivalents of Haste Ye Back came from the wenches.

'Ye cannae beat guid auld Scottish hospitality,' I commented, as we drove back to Glenfinnan. To find that the others were already on their way to Corryhully, a fact witnessed by the unmistakable evidence of the rusting Boomerbus beside the road. There was nothing for it now, and no alternative to uncomfortable donning of apparel in the car, and trudging in their wake. Rivulets running down me, I began to feel that even mud wrestling with an Amazon would be better than this. Little was seen, and less said, till we won to the door of the bothy, Erchie's lamp reflecting in the puddles by the front step.

He and Davie were already bedded against the cold, and we exchanged few comments as we hastened to follow suit. Though Erchie did observe that he doubted the capacity of the fire to add warmth to the next evening's proceedings—our first Burns Supper. I glanced at the strange pillar-box mouth of a fireplace, low down on the wall, and felt he probably had a point. But one that would wait, I thought, as I climbed into my sleeping bag to listen to the wind trying to prise the roof off, the rain rattling and the river's roar. Rising. And to the snores of my companions, who always seemed to fall asleep easier than I did, especially annoying on the occasions I was talking to them.

By morning the storm had abated, but the river had overflowed its banks, and was lapping at the front door of the bothy. The wind was still buffeting, and heavy clouds laboured across the sky. A day to go home if ever there was one, but we could not: the Dominie had indicated that he would come, after his father's funeral. We could not have him stumble on an empty doss, but would have a welcoming fire and party for him. So it was decided: Dave and the Lad—who still had

Munroist ambitions—would go and do Sgurr Thuilm, while Erchie and I, compleat men above (or below) such things, would do Streap.

'Nae because it's a Corbett,' I hastily pointed out, 'but because it's a fine hill.' Davie gave me a silent, knowing look.

Our routes went together up the glen, then forked as our companions began to mount a stalker's path and we carried on to the bealach, which looked down onto Loch Arkaig. The weather had settled now, and become hazily sunny, with occasional sharp flashes of light through cloud breaks. We contoured round to the northern prow of Streap, its classic profile of near-perfect mountain shape providing our route. We had decided this was the proper way to do the hill, do it justice, rather than simply toil up its arse from the bothy. It was cold, and we moved swiftly over the skim of snow and thinly-iced rocks towards the summit.

Attaining it, we looked down on the wild, lonely corrie which is the southern side of the mountain, and along the ridge we would follow back to the bothy. It was cold, but not too cold to admire the drama of the sky, as cloud and shafts of light changed the scene continually behind the static actors in the foreground: the Sgurr of Eigg, Ben Sgritheall, Ladhar Bheinn. One especially sharp shaft of light lit up what looked like a copper cloud, fallen to earth at Strathan below us. I remarked on it to Erchie, who replied:

'That's the roof of the auld school at Strathan, built for the shepherds in Glen Pean and Glen Dessary. A freen o mine went tae it. I'll get ye her address.' We walked southwards along Streap's narrow, but easy, ridge, which led us directly back towards the bothy in the falling darkness, carrying on our backs fallen timber for the fire we hoped to build, and praising ourselves for bringing kindling with us. We changed clothes, made tea, laid out the wood, and waited for our fellows, holding off the fire till their arrival. The rain came on again, and I nipped out by and by to watch the fireflies of their head-torches, slowly descending Sgurr Thuilm, and then bobbing along the path. I put on the kettle again, directed Erchie to begin his pyrolatry , and soon we had company. Wet and tired company.

'See this Munro-baggin, it's murder! Climbin's much less hard work, and ye wouldnae dae it on a day like this. And my bloody knees, they're laupin!' observed Davie on arrival.

I gave him a couple of slugs of Bell's 'Islander', which he took willingly, and a couple of 'Brufen', which he took unwillingly, but soon the aches had been anaesthetised, and he was cheery again, engaging in friendly banter.

'Archie, ye are a disgrace. Yon's no a fire tae greet a man that's been on the hill wi! Corbetteering has corroded ye.'

Now Erchie could light a fire in an Amazonian swamp. He is extremely thorough, and usually starts by rebuilding the fireplace along blast-furnace principles. But he had met his match here—short of demolishing the wall. The fireplace was constructed so that only a little wood could fit in the mouth, and the heat from its combustion went almost exclusively up the chimney. We sat with our feet up the lum, and only about midnight, when the wall had warmed, did any heat emerge from the fireplace. The whisky and the blether warmed us more. But I was determined to go ahead with the Burns Supper.

We started off with half a dozen nips and a toast to the bard in lieu of a proper 'Immortal Memory', which I seemed to remember had originally been the Dominie's remit. Then to the haggis and neeps. I had bought a huge Chieftain, with a proper sheep's pluke, enough to feed an army. But I did overhear Davie saying he had brought his own provisions just in case. The stove was hissing and the neeps and haggis bubbling, Erchie was giving us a few Rabbie sangs, just as a pre-prandial, and everyone seemed to be forgetting the night outside, veritably one on which the De'il might have business on hand. It was a good idea I had had, I thought...

Erchie's song stopped, and so, (I noticed) had the stove. I rushed over: the pluke had burst, and a mass of liquified meal, liver and onions had doused the primus. I confess I swore. Loudly and repeatedly. Erchie and the Lad were silent, possibly suspecting that a hungry night lay ahead of them, but Davie was roaring with laughter.

'It's a judgement! It's a judgement! Trying tae provide themes for bothy week-ends. Ye'll be takkin us tae Theme Parks next, instead o bothies. I'm glad I took my gammon steak.'

I felt like shoving another dozen 'Brufen' down his throat to shut him up—permanently—when the Lad intervened. He extracted the disgusting burst pluke from the pan, and threw it—not, as I had hoped, at Davie—but into the fire. Then he drained the mess in the dixie and dried it out over another stove. And we ate our haggis and neeps—aggressively—under Davie's nose. But without the 'Address to the Haggis', which no one had learned.

At that point the Dominie arrived in the bothy and he was invited in to join the party. Some party, I thought. No 'Immortal Memory', no 'Address to the Haggis', a culinary disaster and a miserable fire. Something had to be done.

Erchie has seldom let me down, and I hoped this would not be an exception. As the Dominie snuggled in to the knot of bodies round the lum, I asked the Boomer for 'Tam o Shanter'. At first he resisted, saying that it was many years since he had recited it, but persistence paid off. By this time we were all pretty fou. I remember there was an Englishman there, who had arrived because his tent had been swept away, though I can't quite remember when he came in. But I do remember his face, struck with amazement, as Erchie recited, almost word-perfect, Burns' magnificent poem in as good a setting as you could get. Amongst a lot of drouthy drunken cronies, and on a night as wild as that described in the poem.

We had a party now. Though only the general outlines of it remain in memory rather than many specific details. There was a lot of singing: good from Erchie and the Dominie, bad from myself though drowned out mostly in chorus lines. I try to practise Safe Singing. As the strains of 'My Love is Like a Red Red Rose' faded, talk got onto the Women Question, and the demand arose for an extempore Address to the Lassies. Somehow, despite my objections that we should at least appoint a quasi-woman to reply for them, I was chosen for this task. Initially reluctant, I warmed to it.

I waded in. It seemed to me that Rabbie had the key to the vexed question of the female mind. There he was, I said, a renowned and successful lecher. Now it wasn't just that he was a good-looking lad, I ventured. It was also his patter that was the key to his success. All this Red Red Rose, and Till the Seas Gang Dry stuff. Now you might think, went my argument, that the lassies were taken in by all this, believed it. Not a chance! They knew fine it was all lies, but it was a payment of the dues necessary. And also something they could pin the blame on the lad with later, even though they had never believed a word of it. I concluded, 'So if ye want yer evil wye, tell them somethin ye baith ken is lees. Rabbie knew the score.'

A heated discussion emerged over this. Erchie thought I was being soft on the Monstrous Regiment, who were temptresses trying to get their hands on your wage-packet. The Dominie, post-macho to the core, defended the Lassies' honour and tried to refute my analysis with the argument that in his school it was the women who recycled aluminium cans, but I didn't quite follow his drift. Davie, high on Bell's and Brufen, shook his head sadly and repeated his favourite line on the issue, 'It's a terrible indictment o wimmen!' This may have been where the altercation with the Englishman began, for I recall demanding that he take an opinion on something, since he had drunk copiously of our whisky, and could not just sit on the fence. Erchie claimed our guest had to be rescued from my wrath, and true enough he must have gotten a fright, for he silently packed and skedaddled when we were all sleeping. The whisky and the miserable lowe of the fire gave out before the issue—whatever it was—was settled.

Next day Davie and Erchie headed back, but the Dominie wanted a walk, and I went with him a little way into the wilds of Loch Shiel. He disappeared into a glorious winter day, to be with his thoughts on the hill, while I sat beside a denuded birch grove, and warmed myself in the glint of sun. I was a bit tired after the strain of being Master of Ceremonies: keeping up the traditions is an exhausting task, I thought, dozing. On first waking I saw a hawk attacking a group of eider-ducks on a little lochan, without success. On second waking I saw the figure of the Dominie returning over the snow-powdered hills.

We drove, silently, back down to Inverarnan for a pint. There we met Wee Onie, Hector and the Auld Crowd, who had had their own Burns Supper in the hotel, and swopped party tales. Then went home with our memories.

But there was still that little matter of the Strathan school...

Echo:
'Lochaber No More'—the Empty Lands of West Arkaig

It is well-known that large areas of the West Highlands were cleared for sheep in the aftermath of the failed rebellion of 1745. One such area was at the west end of Loch Arkaig, in Glens Dessary and Pean, where an observer wrote, 'Families who have not been disturbed for four or five hundred years are turned out of house and home and their possessions given to the highest bidder.' This was in 1804, when the lands belonged to Cameron of Lochiel. Contrary to the romantic Jacobite mythology, Lochiel had had difficulty in raising large numbers of his tenantry for the cause, and some took advantage of the forfeiture of the estate to help the Hanoverian troops burn down Achnacarry House in 1746, and destroy the estate records pertaining to their rents and debts. There was for some years a Hanoverian barracks at the head of Glen Dessary, and General Wade had made a rough road through the glen to Knoydart. But the Redcoats eventually left, and in their place came first Locheil, and then the sheep.

Unlike most West Highland areas, this region did not later convert from sheep run to deer forest, but remained, for a century and a half, one of the biggest sheep farms in the Highlands. In order to run the farm, shepherds had to be brought in, and they occupied half a dozen houses at the loch head, and in the glens running westwards. The O.S. map of 1875 shows them all, and also shows, not a barracks, but a school at Strathan, product of the 1872 Education Act. It was the later replacement of the original school which Erchie had pointed out to me from the summit of Streap. While he tried to locate one of its former scholars, I did a bit of digging in old mountain journals.

The first man to complete his Munros, the Rev. A. E. Robertson, traversed this area at Easter 1895, was given accommodation with two friends at Glen Dessary, and said 'the people in the glen are kind, courteous and hospitable' to walkers. The size of the operation is shown by the fact of the hills carrying 13,000 sheep at this time, and one walker arrived at Strathan in 1908, commenting, 'I came upon a crowd of men clipping sheep and was met by a headlong rush of about twenty dogs.' His name was William Barclay.

After World War I, Glen Dessary was occupied by a family of Stewarts who continued to offer climbers hospitality. One who had been there pre-war noted the changes coming into the area.

> Glen Dessary farm was reached at 5.55. Mrs Stewart told us a hot bath would be ready in half an hour's time. [The bath] had come up by motor launch from the east end of Loch Arkaig. [She] told us that a road was being made along the north side of the loch and that in a year or two Glen Dessary would be in motor communication with the world.

This was in 1926, and the writer, F. S. Goggs, regretted the breaching of isolation the road would entail. Prior to this, apart from when the sheep-drove was accompanied to Spean Bridge, the means of exit and entry was by boat. Up to World War II, supplies were ferried in to the shepherds twice yearly on board the yacht, *Rifle*, from Achnacarry, although the recent road brought the post-van twice a week, and the possibility of its utilisation as passenger transport. Another regular visitor to the area was the Rev. Burn, second man to complete his 'Munros'. He usually lodged with the Stewarts at Strathan. He spoke most warmly of the hospitality of his hosts, and the help given him in his studies of Gaelic place-names and in song-collection by the family up to the early 1920s. As this book was going to press, there appeared Elizabeth Allan's *Burn on the Hill* (Bidean) which gives much information on 'Wee Ronnie's' wanderings in this and other areas of the Highlands.

The yacht Rifle—main means of supply to the shepherds of Glen Dessary by Loch Arkaig

Another house serving a shepherd's family was in Glen Pean. Built in 1894, it replaced a house on the opposite bank of the river, which was twice almost swept away in landslides! It was occupied by a family of Campbells (who had seven children) until 1915 when they vacated it. Mr Campbell had moved to Glen Pean in 1870 and his daughter Lexie recalled that he was often away for days gathering the sheep. He was a writer of Gaelic songs and poems, and all the children had only Gaelic when they went to school—to which they had to walk daily three miles down the glen to Strathan. Lexie recalled her days there:

> We had many happy days at Glen Pean...I see Mother coming down the glen to meet us, carrying our dinners and getting us to help her to lift the peats. Some of us would bring the cattle home and mother would be helped by one of the girls to milk the cows.

I had put all this aside, when my friend phoned. He gave me a number which I called, and I found myself talking to someone born—not at Glen Pean—but at A' Chuil, another shepherd's cottage opposite Glen Dessary. Lorna McGibbon had been born in 1939, in the house her parents—the Sutherlands from Stratherrick—had previously moved into. She told me there was bothy accommodation for the single shepherds at Strathan, and when married they moved into one of the houses. Though only four when she left, she remembered cows being swum across the river, calves downstream, and the hay-making at A' Chuil. And she supplied me with some moving old photographs of her birthplace—as well as the telephone number of a Peter Cameron, whose family had occupied the house at Strathan.

I had a long chat with Peter, now in his seventies and retired in Dunfermline. His family were Lochaber people, who had occupied the house in Glen Kingie, to the north of Strathan (then also part of the Locheil sheep-farm), until 1941. Then his family had moved to Strathan, and he had left the area. I asked about the school—another blank, since they had had a resident school teacher at Glen Kingie for the Cameron children, the track over to Strathan being too long and rough for the children to use daily. But he did tell me that the building also doubled up as a church, with occasional visits by an outside minister. Ceilidhs, I asked? Oh, yes, there were plenty of them, but they took place in a sheep-shed at Strathan itself. The school, he thought, closed around 1950, just after his family left Strathan. He did not remember many climbers and walkers in the area in the 1930s, but said there were still many travelling people, who turned up at the isolated shepherd's houses such as Glen Kingie. Today, Glen Kingie is a mountain bothy, restored from the ruinous state it fell into after 1941. The same has happened to A' Chuil and Glen Pean. The less isolated Strathan continued as a sheep-farm longer than the other habitations, but eventually —like Murlaggan and Upper Glendessary, two other shepherd's houses —became a holiday home. Kinlocharkaig, at the south side of the loch, was spared that fate, and simply became a ruin. Like the school...

That school was proving a problem. It had been in the old Inverness Division, so I wrote to Highland Regional Council, which informed me they could 'find no trace of such an establishment'! But eventually a letter came from Skye (in reply to an enquiry of mine in the *West Highland Free Press*) with help from Miss Connie MacInnes. Her father, from Ord, had been one of the fourteen shepherds on the farm at Upper Glendessary in the 1930s. The school, which she had attended, was reputedly the smallest—in physical dimensions—in Britain! There were eight scholars in the thirties—and nearly two dozen in the 1920s. One of its products was Norman Maclean, singer and mod gold medallist. Connie's teachers had been Skye women, and had lodged with the parents' families. She remembered the glen warmly. As well as ceilidhs, there was an annual dance in the sheep-shed, and the children had a party at Christmas. Connie also provided me with an old photo of the *Rifle* at a flitting.

Now the fiery cross was going round Skye! I got a letter from Mrs Maisie Nicolson, daughter of the Glendessary Stewarts. Her father had been head shepherd under Locheil. She enclosed a copy from an old *Life and Work* of an article by Mr Whalley, a student missionary in Arkaig from 1933-41. He had preached to a congregation of 35 in the corrugated iron schoolhouse:

> Some came on foot, one young shepherd on a motor cycle, others on push cycles, in the keeper's car, the folk from the most isolated glen on horseback, some from across the loch by rowing boat...

Whalley visited Glen Kingie, six miles over a high pass, to give the five Cameron children Sunday school—they saw so few strangers they ran away from the minister on his first visit! Even the G.P.O. refused to deliver to Glen Kingie, and paid one of the boys to come out and collect the family letters. I hoped that Locheil had improved Glen Kingie cottage since it was visited by the Rev. Burn when occupied by the MacLeans in the 1920s. He described it thus:

> I got a warm welcome from Mrs MacLean, her usual kind self. She told me that this house was ruinous when she came in, with no doors that would

shut, no window frames or glass. Water comes in up the hearthstone [and] the plaster is breaking away from the walls.

At the bottom of Whalley's article a scribbled note said that Professor William Barclay had also been a missionary at the Strathan school. The same man who was there in 1908, I wondered?

Maisie confirmed that Gaelic was universal in West Arkaig in the 1930s—except at school, where it was never spoken, despite the teachers having Gaelic! There was no evacuation of the area, but the effects of the war led to families gradually moving out.

This was not the end of the Skye connection, however: another letter arrived, from the daughter of *another* Skye shepherd, William Douglas. Now a young lad of 89, he had been a shepherd at A' Chuil for 15 years pre-war. His daughter told me her uncle had had his wedding reception at Strathan:

> The barn was all cleared out and decorated for the occasion, and friends came from all around and had a great day. The glen was a very busy place at that time.

Although many families moved out, some houses were still occupied after the war, when sheep-farming was continued on a reduced scale. David Cameron and his father Angus Hugh worked out of Glendessary in the late fifties and early sixties, when there were still 10,000 sheep and eleven shepherds on the estate; but interestingly, there were no children in the school by then.

Today there is an air of sadness about Loch Arkaig, with only holiday homes and ruins, where formerly there were communities. This is compounded by the monotony of the conifers which choke both Glen Pean and Dessary, for these lands were sold for private forestry some time ago. It is no longer true that, as the old saying went,'Everything you can see is Locheil's, and everything you can't see is Locheil's also.'

Sheep farming did not prove an economically viable use of mountain land, and neither, one feels, would monocultural forestry but for the tax-breaks and subsidies involved. There is good land at the west end of Loch Arkaig, and in no other country than Scotland would one find it devoid of people. The trouble was, that by the time such legislation as the Crofters Acts was passed, there were no crofters here. For them it had been exile, and 'Lochaber No More', as it was to be later for the shepherds of Locheil. Through my investigations, I feel I know them, people I have never met. I have tramped their hills, and slept on the floors of their abandoned dwellings: hopefully this repays the debt a little.

February:
THE GALLOWA HILLS

Davie's scepticism was his usual, and on this occasion vindicated, counterpoint to my idealistic schemes. I give a synthesis of his varied points of opposition.

'It's sooth, it's the wrang wye. We'll get lost. It's no traditional, and there's no hills there.'

'Aye there is, Corbetts,' was my reply.

'That's no hills,' was his.

But he came anyway, and I picked him up in Milngavie. He assured me he knew a 'quick way' to Cumbernauld, and thence by the A74 to Galloway, and I deferred to him. I have found that even post-macho men are touchy about their cars, their driving and their sense of direction in roughly that order. So I followed his barked out directions as he fumed again against this whole Gallovidian muddle. Davie is like a dog with a bone: you can never get him off it, unless you throw another, so I did.

'Got the Garden Gnome oot yet?'

It took an inordinate time, the longest short-cut in the world, to get to Cumbernauld, most of which Davie spent proving that the Gnome was a gift, and that he had no intention of transforming it from a baby bath-toy to a garden ornament.

There appeared to be no directions out of Cumbernauld: maybe nobody ever left it. Or went there. But Davie seemed to know the way, and we meandered through the dark February night until we had been well over an hour from Milngavie. Enough time to get to Galloway, I thought. Then we had to admit we were lost. Somewhere in Lanarkshire where the only people going anywhere know the way, and don't need direction signs. I decided to stop and ask a knot of young girls and a boy where we were as Davie studied the road map fruitlessly. I addressed the question to the lad.

'I not know...I not understand...Sorree...'

'Cheeky bastard,' I said to Davie, 'Takkin a rise oot o us...'

The lassies had heard us and intervened to save the lad's honour.

They were schoolgirls, he the local school's French assistant—hence his success with the opposite sex. Gallic charm. And they told us where we were. Bellshill.

'Bellshill, by Christ!' uttered Davie. 'Quick, run the windae up and get oot o here. The land o Rottweilers and Prejudice. We are lookin for Backhill o the Bush and we find Bellshill o the Lodge. I said nae good would come o goin sooth...'

We escaped, eventually finding the A74 and adjusting our mental lodestones south. I passed the time telling Davie it wouldn't be too bad...There were nice wee Corbetts for a winter's day, I had lent Erchie a tape of 'The Gallowa Hills' to learn, so we could keep up the traditions, and finally the lad I had phoned told me Backhill was a nice wee cosy bothy, and he had just renovated it before leaving the country for a couple of years. Dave was mollified—more so by the pint we had time to drink before closing at New Galloway, where we picked up a couple of workmates on their first bothy trip. We had arranged to meet another quartet of people at the bothy: they would already be there, I thought.

But we did it again. There were excuses. It was one of the blackest nights I have ever seen, though we had the Land Rover track all the way, which possibly made us careless. And I had the map, and Davie the compass (or the other way round) which was careless too. But to this day Davie swears it was more the disorientation brought about by going south, turning our normal homing instincts upside down. For we got lost again, missing a very obvious turn-off to our right.

We carried on regardless, assuring our two colleagues that, having gone four miles, it was only a couple to go to the cosy wee bothy. Then there was a sliver of silver to our right: too big for the river. A loch? But we should pass no loch...Consultations, recriminations—and three miles back to the turn-off, with another five to go after that. At 3 a.m. we got to Backhill, set back in a forest clearing. And we only found it because Erchie had left his Diogenes Lamp, his Tilly, on for us. It may never show an honest man, but the Tilly showed us the way to Backhill, shafting a pin-prick in the pitch-black void.

'Christ, nae wonder yon lad left the country,' came from Davie, crossing the threshold in front of me, 'this place is a pit!'

As I followed, even the weak light from Erchie's Tilly showed Davie to have indulged in no hyperbole. Morning would reveal more dereliction, but dark night showed the doorless doss to be largely windowless as well, with a broken staircase leading to an upper floor below a roof of a thousand drips. We barely had time to mumble thanks to Erchie for his lamp before hiding from the horror in our sleeping bags, twisting to avoid drips and draughts.

For the rain had started, and continued all next day. It was mild, wet and windy. The original plan had been the Rinns of Kells, the Corbetteers' Cuillin, but that was out of the question. While we pondered on an alternative we collected wood for the evening and examined the bothy surroundings. All sorts of debris lay scattered around—and inside—the bothy, which had no doors and hardly a window. It was too miserable a place to hang about all day, so at about twelve we opted for Corserine, the highest point of the Rinns; plodded along a track, buffetted up a fire-break in the forest, staggered in wind and mist to the summit. Turned round, took a compass bearing, and came back. En route we saw nothing but a herd of old goats, who looked at us in that surprised way goats do. They probably hadn't expected to see another herd.

Back at Backhill darkness covered the worst of its eyesores, and the business of eating and warmth took minds off the rest. The fire was at first a problem. The wood was wet and the lum was bad, thus a debate took place between Erchie and Davie—both old Steelmen—as to whether the Open Hearth or the Bessemer Converter method of igniting it was best. For a while that gave out more heat than the fire. Others were occupied in removing wet clothes and preparing meals, even though it was early. I decided to give up my primus to one of the novices: I felt sorry that his first bothy was such a pit (he has never been bothying again). I made the offer, politely, that he could be primus with my stove.

'Oh, no thanks,' he replied, 'I never eat till later, maybe 8 o'clock, at home.'

(It was about four o'clock.)

'You are not at home,' I replied, 'but in a bothy. It is cold and you are wet. You should change and eat, and by that time Erchie will have us all roasting.'

I probably sounded too schoolmasterish for a colleague's ears. And habits acquired on the sun and sangria soaked beaches of Spain proved resistant to change on one bothy trip. He sat there, remaining as cheerful as possible while we all crammed hot carbohydrates down our throats, and Erchie began to get a response from his loving foreplay with the fire. The steam was rising from our continental diner, and I noticed he was beginning to chitter, and cast inquiring looks at the clutter of stoves on the table. Around half past five he asked, as casually as possible, 'Any of those stoves vacant yet?'—and space was knowingly made for him.

And indeed Erchie soon had the fire in the Backhill of the Bush more like the Biblical Burning Bush: *Nec Tamen Consumebatur*—it gave out inordinate amounts of heat with little apparent sustenance. Despite the fact that gales were blowing (you could not call them draughts) through the door and the windows—not to mention down the stairs— we were warm in all but isolated parts of our anatomies. Mr 10% told the story of the Gorilla and the Nun for those who hadn't heard it. Davie found a new angle on Starvation Gulch and the Women Question. The Dominie untangled the Gordian knot of Galloway place-names for us, and Erchie had learned a few new songs, including one whose chorus we all—whisky having overcome our afternoon feelings—joined in with a will.

Oh, the Gallowa hills are covert wi broom,
Wi heather bells and bonnie doon,
Wi heather bells and riveries a',
And I'll gang oot oer the hills tae Gallowa.

On the way out the road seemed long enough, even without our enforced diversion of Friday night. A long walk through serried ranks of pines that blotted out the view in any direction. But a little diversion was provided once back at the car when we saw a herd of Gallowa 'belties', the small tapir-like cattle of the region, which delighted Davie especially. Maybe he is closer to nature now he has his garden, I thought.

But it was a lot of effort and discomfort for a coo and a Corbett— even with the song. I feel we might have made a hasty judgement based on one trip, but we have not been back to Galloway. I have to agree with Davie, that there is something unnatural about going south.

Echo:
From the Cuillin to Kirkcudbright

He too had made a mistake in going to Galloway. Here is his story, one of under-fulfilled talent.

A Skyeman who left his mark, not only on the social and cultural history of the Gael, but also on the development of mountaineering on the island, who spent his prime in the alien Gallowa lands. Alexander Nicolson, who was born at Husabost and died in Edinburgh, is well known for his quatrain:

> Jerusalem, Athens and Rome,
> I would see them before I die;
> But I'd rather not see any one of these three
> Than be exiled for ever from Skye.

—similar to the panegyrics composed on most Hebridean islands by exiled Gaels. But his extraordinarily full and varied life contained much more of note.

Nicolson's father was the proprietor of Husabost, and his early education was from private tutors. He went to Edinburgh University, intending to enter the Free Kirk ministry, and graduated B.A. in 1850, but he abandoned the study of theology and spent the next decade at various posts. For a while he lectured in logic and philosophy at the University, later being one of the sub-editors of the *Encyclopaedia Britannica*. He edited the *Edinburgh Guardian* and later the *Daily Express*, which, despite the name, was a paper of radical Liberal affiliations, a philosophy Nicolson remained true to all his life, though defecting to Chamberlain's Liberal Unionists over opposition to Irish Home Rule.

Neither his journalistic nor his academic career really took off, and in 1860 he was called to the Bar, again without much impact. He had little business, and made ends meet by legal journalism, as well as publishing articles and poems in the *Scotsman* and the *Gael*. Finally he was appointed Sheriff-substitute at Kirkcudbright in 1872, whence he transferred in the same post to Greenock in 1885, retiring on grounds of ill-health four years later. Again, hardly a meteoric success story. When he died he left his estate of £762 to his sister who lived with him in Edinburgh—a modest middle-class legacy.

What is intriguing about Nicolson is that—just at the time when he was appointed to Kirkcudbright—he turned down the offer of the Celtic Chair at Edinburgh University, which Professor Blackie had been largely instrumental in founding. This is surprising, since as well as being a renowned Greek scholar, Nicolson was regarded as one of the foremost Gaelic experts of his day. As well as his own verses, which are of interest rather than merit, he published in 1882 *A Collection of Gaelic Proverbs and Familiar Phrases*, and he was the man the SPCK asked to revise the translation of the Gaelic Bible. His otherwise eulogistic obituary in the

Scotsman stated that 'he was of a lethargic constitution, which impaired his energy': possibly he preferred the under-employed life of a sheriff-substitute, supplemented by journalism, to that of academia? Certainly Nicolson, who was the epitome of the 'convivial' bachelor, and who was a popular figure in society, seemed to put more effort into his enthusiasms for his Highland Volunteer activities in Edinburgh, his playing of shinty, and his membership of the Edinburgh Highland societies, than into his career!

If Nicolson's life-story does suggest that of a man who found it hard to settle and concentrate his talents on one vocation, when it came to matters concerning the Gael and Skye, then energy was certainly not wanting! Many will know that he was one of the six experts appointed to serve under Lord Napier in his eponymous Commission of 1883-4 enquiring into the causes of the crofters' agitation on the western seaboard. Nicolson spent several months (and survived the sinking of the Commissioners' boat, the *Lively* in Stornoway harbour) working on the report which laid the basis for the later Crofters' Act of 1886. But he had already served in a similar capacity in 1865, when appointed to the Scottish Education Commission to visit virtually all the inhabited western islands and to report on the state of their schools. His report, published as a parliamentary 'blue book', is regarded as a model of its kind, and helped lay the basis for the Education Act of 1872.

It was these journeys which gave Nicolson the opportunity to compare his native isle with the other Hebrides he had visited. This he did with generosity, though ultimately, I would imagine, to the agreement of none bar his fellow Sgitheanaich.

Mull has beauty and grandeur…
Jura—Queenly in state, but lacks variety
Tiree—too flat, but many charms
Barra—rough and rocky
Lewis—boggy
Harris—almost like Skye in mountain grandeur
Staffa and Iona—a universal sense of wonder
Skye—Queen of them all.

It was in this same year of his travels as an education commissioner that Nicolson's mountaineering career began. When Nicolson visited Sligachan in 1865, the Cuillin were still virtually *terra incognita*. True, Professor Forbes had made the first recorded ascent of Sgurr nan Gillean in 1836, and produced the first reasonably accurate sketch-map of the Cuillin after a repeat ascent in 1845. But, leaving aside Bla Bheinn which

On the Skye Ridge

had been ascended in 1857 by the poet Swinburne, only Bruach na Frithe, climbed by Forbes in 1845, and Sgurr a' Ghreadaidh, ascended by John Mackenzie in 1870, had been climbed of the eleven peaks on the main ridge. After making the fourth recorded ascent of Sgurr nan Gillean, Nicolson, without proper maps and equipment, but showing a remarkable pioneering skill, was to double the number of Cuillin peaks conquered by 1874. He was accompanied by the Sligachan gamekeeper, Duncan MacIntyre, but was clearly the leader in all the expeditions undertaken.

After showing his pioneering talents by ascending Sgurr nan Gillean by a new route ('Nicholson's Chimney'), the Sheriff decided to branch out. The usual access points for the Cuillin at that time were Sligachan and Coruisk—the latter by boat. Nicolson ventured one day into Coire Lagain and obtained a glimpse of a fine peak, which he decided to climb. The next day he set off, ascending Sgurr na Banachdich first. He passed by the Inaccessible Pinnacle, today the most prized of all Munros, and observed that 'with ropes and grappling irons one might be able to overcome it'. But he left it well alone and, wisely, on coming to a trickier part of the ridge, descended into Coire Lagain, and then re-ascended to the summit, subsequently called Sgurr Alasdair, by the route known as the Great Stone Shoot. He observed, 'We did it without much difficulty, one or two places requiring a good grip of hands and feet, but on the whole I have seen worse places.'

This peak was, several years later, found by Norman Collie to be the highest point on the whole Cuillin, replacing Sgurr Dearg. But Nicolson's greatest mountaineering achievement was his ascent and traverse of Sgurr Dubh in the next year of 1874, described by Ben Humble in his *The Cuillin of Skye* as 'the finest thing done in climbing in Britain up till that time.' Had he joined the Alpine Club he might have ranked as one of the great Victorian mountaineers, but he was interested only in his native Cuillin.

Nicolson and a friend had visited Coruisk on a fine day. The barometer was set fair and there was to be a full moon. At four o'clock they started up towards Sgurr Dubh, and after some difficult scrambling reached the top at seven, when dark was falling (it was September). They now faced the problem of descent in the dark over unknown ground, and started off over the steep rocks and wet slabs towards Coruisk. Nicolson described his unusual tactics in the descent—but as all climbers know, *in extremis* 'anything goes':

My companion, being the lighter man, stood above, with his heels well set in the rock, holding the plaid by which I let myself down the chasm. Having got footing, I rested my back against the rock down which my lighter friend let himself slide till he rested on my shoulder.

Repeating this stratagem they eventually reached Coruisk and crossed Druim Hain towards Sligachan, which they finally gained at 3 a.m. Though he did no more first ascents in the Cuillin, Nicolson did much to publicise Skye as a mountaineering mecca by his articles in various journals, particularly a series in 1875 on the island in *Good Words*, a magazine with a national rather than Scottish circulation edited by Dr Norman Macleod, the Queen's chaplain. This and the opening of the railway to Strome Ferry meant that in the 1880s the Cuillin had as many ascents in an average week as it had had in the previous half-century, as the luminaries of the Alpine Club like the Pilkington Brothers and Norman Collie scaled its summits. Indeed it was they who insisted on naming the highest point on the island after Nicolson: he had modestly suggested Sgurr Lagain. The sheriff continued to visit Skye every other year, commenting 'here a day is worth two in most places.' The thousands of mountaineers who have followed since in his footsteps would doubtless agree with him—with all due respect to Gallowa.

March:
EASTER ISLANDS

We decided on them as Erchie had never been there—a teenage trip to Great Bernera forty years before excepted. And there was always the Clisham as well, its slopes untrodden by either him or the Dominie. And en route I had a reading and slide show to give at an Inverness Walking Club, where I would earn a few pieces of silver towards the expenses of the trip itself. We were burdened mentally and weakened physically by the gloomy rigours of a Scottish winter, and were hoping this would be a minor rebirth.

But the day before departure, I was informed that a club member had been killed on a club outing, and to be prepared for a leaden occasion. They stood talking in distracted knots as I got ready, and one or two had bruises whose origin I did not enquire into. I tried: reading a couple of passages where I had attempted to convey the consolations of mountaineering, and showing some slides of another man's great days on the hill. By the end I had provided some diversion, the only comfort I could offer. The ceremony seemed to solemnify death without offering any hope of resurrection.

Nor did the weather offer us much hope, as we battled through the wind and rain on Skye, from where the ferry battered through the choppy Minch to Harris, on a day when it was so dark one might have believed the earth had missed an orbit. We drove on to Rhenigidale, to the hostel, and to three days of the worst weather I have ever witnessed. Though the rain was intermittent, gale force winds were constant, and mixed with hail and sleet. The smothered tops, we were told, were still snow-covered on an island which hardly sees snow at all.

But it was a long way to come for nothing, so we drove around in the squalls, showing Erchie the wonders of the island. At Callanish we head-butted the wind round the stones, while a bus load of German tourists waited for it to abate before following us: they were waiting when we left. At Rodel Kirk we came across a BBC film-crew abandoning an attempt to film, as their sound and umbrellas were wind-carried away. Despite our disappointment at the weather, we had to work very hard not to be awed by the flowing manes of the waves crashing on the deserted beaches of Harris, or the cloud convulsions over the moors at Achmore. And my companions surely could not help but be impressed, as I was.

And we skirmished with the superior forces of the weather, engaged it in guerrilla combat, winning no wars but raising morale. Erchie was nursing a wounded knee, and dropped us off the first day to toddle up Toddun, a 1,700 ft arched eminence behind Rhenigidale, where we ambushed the wind on the way up, and retreated before its awakened fury on the way down. Next day we walked from Tarbert to our hostel on the four mile road constructed by the villagers as a cart-track when Rhenigidale was the last roadless village in Britain. It was extremely well-made, with 'cassies'—cobblestones—battered into the peaty earth as it climbed to 900 ft, dropped to sea level and then climbed over another hill of 300 ft to the village, all by a series of well-constructed zig-zag bends.

At Loch Trollamarig the road served another village, Moliginish, only abandoned in 1965. Rhenigidale, which once had ninety people, only narrowly escaped that fate. About thirty were evacuated after World War I to Portnalong in Skye, a government-assisted weavers' development, and by the time the road came in 1989 there were only five occupied houses, and two children. Even in the sixties the authorities were trying to offer evacuation as an alternative to building a road. The locals, unlike those who visited the place before the road, had no love of their primitive isolation. A friend had been there in the seventies and told me one complaint he heard was, 'if anyone is ill, we have to take them out on the sick-sack.' Puzzled, he asked if this was a special amphibious stretcher. 'No, the sick-sack. The road. We have to carry them out,' was the reply.

But even with the road, the assortment of young Australians and—mostly—young Germans who had made their way to the hostel found the place wondrous beyond compare, epic in its majesty. One young German was thunderstruck, when walking past a Lewis church, to hear the hypnotic, nasal rise and fall of the Psalm singing. He sat down outside to listen to the music, whose existence he had been unaware of.

'It's all right for them,' said Erchie, 'but we've a Corbett tae do. I vote we try and grab it on the wye tae the ferry the morra.'

We said we would let the weather decide. But we did not.

We were sitting in a lay-by at one side of the road, the other side of its tarmac strip barely visible in the mist and rain. The car was rocking in the wind. The Dominie and I had decided to defer to the authority of the weather—but not the Boomer himself. He lodged an appeal.

'It's taen me fifty years tae get here. I might no get back, probably won't. I've tae think like that noo. I want tae dae it.'

When a man who has breasted 20,000 ft on three continents wants to breast 2,000 on Harris, honour bids you follow. We put on our boots and waterproofs. Silently.

The holiday did not end there. We moved on to South Uist, Erchie and I, (with the Dominie following us, in order—going by the convoluted Cal-Mac timetable—to get back to Skye and head home). So there was more to come, and I will merely say that the ascent of Clisham was an interminable plod over grass and boulders, through mist and rain, to the ridge. Then another head-down struggle to the summit through deep snow, avoiding heavy cornicing to our right. The mist was slashed momentarily at the top, showing Seaforth Island eastwards, and westwards the empty moorlands rolling towards Loch Resort. In the brief eating respite on the top, I told the Mafia about my trip there the previous summer, and about the deserted village at Kinlochresort. But it was no time for ethnology, and we descended, Erchie slowly. Protecting his knee.

We got back down. Erchie had won his Battle of Wounded Knee. But as I say, the holiday did not end there: there was more—and worse—to come.

A couple of days later we were sitting in the hostel at Howmore on the Sabbath. Outside, sleet, snow and rain. Inside, washing, eating, resting. Tending the fire and tidying up. Noticing that the doss was in a bad way. Lath and plaster flaking off, the thackit roof leaking, and the pervasive dampness only driven away by the lowe of the flames in the stove. It was a day when even going outside the front door was out of the question. The old shepherd had told us when we arrived that he had never known such a spring for wind and cold. The lambs were dying, the ground still unsown—for here in Uist is virtually the last place crofters still till the land and grow crops on the sandy machair fields.

So we stayed in, talking to a lassie left behind by a work-party which had started building temporary shelter in an old byre, so that the hostel could be overhauled. She was an expert dry-stane dyker, mountain path repairer, and was musical. She was also pretty and vivacious. In addition, she told us she was a senior engineer on transatlantic container ships. Erchie was puzzled, and said, 'Is that no a funny job for a lassie?'

Monklands is traditional. It is no wonder they called their leisure centre the Time Capsule: the whole place is one. Hairy arsed Tims battle with hairy chested Prods of a Friday night, and for women it's still *Kinder, Kirche, Kuche*. Maybe a little of that has rubbed off on the Boomer. But not on this lassie. Nor on the German quine who arrived later, and with whom we finished a German crossword after midnight. She read the clues in German, I translated for Erchie, he gave the answer and I and the German re-translated Erchie's answers to fit the available space.

And we told a story, competing with the howl of the hurricane outside Howmore. As I said, we did not go outside that day. But we had been out the day before. And we told them about it.

It had cleared and Hecla was visible. Not the active volcano at nearly 5,000 ft in Iceland, once reputed to be the entry to Hell, but the eponymous modest peak on Uist, just failing to breach the 2,000 ft contour. The worst Easter in living memory had given us gales and blizzards on the Clisham of Harris but now our luck seemed to have turned. The bad weather had headed for Skye, the hills were clear under powder snow and out to the Atlantic it was—at last—cloudless.

'We'll go for Hecla, and then see,' I suggested to Erchie, who agreed. I was hoping it would stay settled for the entire ridge to Beinn Mhor. The traverse of Uist's three peaks gives a fine long day, over wild terrain with spectacular views in all directions.

Local knowledge. Leaving the thatched hostel at Howmore we called on the warden at the road end. Since my visit twenty years ago, all the thatched cottages had been vacated, and the village moved to new houses by the main road. One of them, however, was maintained by the Gatliffe Trust as a bunkhouse somewhere between bothy and Youth Hostel standards.

'It should stay clear today,' suggested Mrs MacDonald, and we set off in sunshine. Check conditions. An English lad staying at the hostel, repairing dry stane dykes, had had problems with river crossings, so we kept high, traversing Haarsal and a host of other mounds, before coming to the slopes below Maoil Daimh—one of the few Gaelic place names amongst ubiquitous Norse nomenclature. Norway ruled here till the late thirteenth century.

It had been clear and sunny, and below us we could see clusters of chambered cairns and Loch Druidibeg, where the swans and geese were gathering to begin breeding. But spring was late, and so was their nesting, as were the lambing and the ploughing of the machair for the crops.

'We might be lucky and get a view,' I suggested.

The first (fairly brief) squall came in, visible for miles away out to the Atlantic before it hit. It passed over, and behind it the coppery light played a dazzling game with the mirrors of sea and sky. The second squall was longer and was full of snow as we toiled up the slopes of an invisible Hecla.

'Maybe it's in for the day,' suggested Erchie, but he was contradicted before he finished speaking by a band of metallic light at the horizon, which soon extended to a new period of brightness. We saw Hecla again, and Ben Corodale, and Beinn Mhor, under a full covering of snow, looking like something misplaced from Arctic regions. I was now sure we would get the whole ridge done, in fine conditions.

There had been wind all day, and it became stiffer crossing a long plateau to the final 300 ft or so of the hill. But it was not buffeting, and leaning against it we made good progress. I just caught a glimpse of the uninhabited east coast of Uist, before the mist came down, with some sleet for its companion. The wind rose as we rose.

I've been in wind before: head down, legs apart, lean into it, and on you go. Sometimes I've had to go on all fours, and once had to crawl. I went straight up where a faint path led, Erchie dropped a few feet off the ridge, hoping for shelter. But this wind came from all directions. It seemed to corkscrew round the mountain, making it impossible to use rocks for shelter. Well, they would do for handholds, I thought as I stooped first to all fours and then onto my belly. I could not see Erchie. I shouted, realised he would not hear over the howl of the wind, and reassured myself.

'He's gone down,' I thought, recalling that his knee had been troubling him, and he had said he might opt out.

I crawled up a little ramp and was on the summit ridge, the top maybe twenty feet away in distance, less in height. The wind rolled me over like a log, and I clawed back upwards, to be lifted bodily off the ground, and rolled over again. All around was milky mist, hail was stinging my face and eyes. I gripped onto the rocks and waited for the wind to drop. It was getting cold, colder. The wind did not drop. I looked at the summit: I could have thrown a rock to it, almost spat on it, had the weather not been as it was. Unlike its namesake, this Hecla was a cold Hell.

'It's not even 2,000 ft,' I thought, which added to the indignity, and made retreat seem unjustifiable. The top was a rocky plug, falling maybe 50 ft on three sides.

'Far enough,' was my decision.

I crawled forward again, was wind-rolled a little further this time, and, when breath was regained, slithered downhill head-first on my belly for a couple of hundred feet, smoothing out the footsteps of my ascent with the snake-mark of my retreat. The only other time I've descended a hill head-first was when avalanched.

I put it to the back of my mind until I was safely down below the summit, and could stand up, check my compass. I had seen no footsteps of Erchie's in the snow.

'He must be down, he can't possibly be up there.'

I hesitated, then took a few steps.

'I'll go as far as that cairn we had a snack at, and see if I can pick up his footprints.'

But the snow had gone as fast as it had come, and did not resolve my doubts. I was now below the mist, scanned the moor and saw nothing but moor.

'If he had turned back, he'd have…half an hour up, the same down…an hour's start. He could be down at the loch by now. Probably waiting for me there.'

The tops remained out of sight in clouds moving in a mad stampede across them. The rain came on, advancing in ordered columns joining sea and sky, covering the moor. I got to the loch. He was not there.

'He must be down. He's back at the car, probably frozen waiting. He can't have moved that fast, he must still be up there? I left him on the mountain. I'll have to go back up…But he's an experienced mountaineer: he would know to get down. Maybe he has come down the other side…'

A blue dot bobbing against the grey of the rain and the dull green of the moor. About a mile away. Thank fuck. Stupid fears. Do something. Eat a Mars Bar and drink a can of Irn-Bru. Already my worry seems unreal…and was the wind all that bad? I had time to get cold again before he arrived. Let him speak first.

'That was fucking awful. I've been out in wind, but that was a hurricane. I was clutching rocks on my belly and thought the wind would lift me over the edge.'

After a pause, he added,

'I was a wee bit worried. I thought I might have left ye there, wasn't sure you were down. But then I thought, he's an experienced mountaineer, he'll know to get down, even if maybe not exactly the way we came up.'

I felt a surge of warmth for him, that blocked out for a minute the penetrating cold of the rain and wind.

We trudged back over the moor and under the rain to the hostel. The stove we had banked up needed only a rake to burst into flame. In the evening another of what the Gaels call turadh—a gap between the showers—occurred and the hills were bathed in cold sunshine, devoid of snow under a clear sky. Our Hell on Hecla was now only memory, fading in the wake of the melted snow.

'Folk wouldn't believe that if ye told them,' commented Erchie, adding, 'I don't know if I believe it myself now.'

'Did ye get to the tap?' I asked, having forgotten to.

'Oh, aye,' he said, 'I might never be here again so I'd no choice.'

Then he added,

'But I nearly didn't get back.'

And we left it at that.

We were lucky with the ferries. The three days we crossed from island to island we had a following wind: the other days of the week contrary winds kept the boats in port. From the rain-lashed deck I looked back towards South Uist, to Hecla where we had fallen, and risen.

Echo:
The Last Deserted Village?

The cases of St Kilda and to a lesser extent Scarp are well-known ones of Highland settlements evacuated within living memory: examples of the long, slow attrition which contributed as much to Highland depopulation as the infamous Clearances of the last century.

However, tucked away in the wilds between the mountains of Harris and the Uig hills of Lewis was a lesser-known settlement, Kinresort or Ceannreasort, which is possibly the last of the deserted villages, the final inhabitant departing only thirty years ago. Though not an island, like St Kilda or Scarp, Kinresort was extremely remote, never having a road to it, and connected to the outside world by a five-mile walk over a literally trackless moor of extreme roughness and wetness, or a doubly long and tricky sail to the end of Loch Resort from the road at Hushinish—itself miles from anywhere.

Apparently in the middle of the nineteenth century a road into Kinresort was begun, but Donald Munro, hated factor of the then owner of Lewis and Harris, Sir James Matheson (who bought the island with money made in the opium trade), persuaded him to halt the work, since a road might have spoiled the shooting in the area.

That there had traditionally been some settlement at Kinresort is shown by Hunter's map of 1826, where a habitation is marked at Longhar, at the east end of the loch. Longhar, or Luachair, may have been the house of the Harris gamekeeper, or possibly a shepherd. Later a small shooting lodge, known as the Iron House, was built on the Harris side of the Kinresort river, but this was destroyed by fire and derelict by the turn of the century. My own archaeological investigations found Glasgow-made bricks dated 1851 in the rubble of the ruin, which may provide a clue to its construction by the Earl de Grey, who at that time rented the Harris shooting and fishing.

The Kinresort river separates Lewis and Harris, and also divides Kinresort itself: Crola, or Croleatha (broad sheepfold) lies on the Lewis side, and Luachair (the rushy place) on the Harris side. Only with local government reorganisation in the 1970s did Lewis and Harris come under a common administration—though as we shall see, this separation did not seem to hinder co-operation between those who lived at Kinresort.

On the Crola side there stood a keeper's cottage built about 1850, which by the 1880s was occupied by a family of Mackenzies who had come there from Wester Ross. On the same side of the river, from 1861, lived a family of MacDonalds originally cleared from Scarp. They were the longest resident family, staying there for a hundred years.

On the Luachair side there was also a keeper's cottage, the best preserved building left today, as well as a pair of thatched cottages by the river. These seem to have been established by families cleared from Scarp in 1885—another group of MacDonalds, related to the Crola ones, and the Mackaskills. This picture of the settlement is confirmed by the unpublished autobiography of A. J. Mackenzie, born at Kinresort in 1887:

> Including ourselves [Kinresort] comprised five families. Three of the families were on the Harris side, and two—ourselves and Crola—on the Lewis side.

The establishment of a community in such a remote location, and at such a late date, is a testimony to the terrible land-hunger in Lewis, which saw its population increase by 300 per cent in the last century, to almost 30,000, while that of other islands such as Skye, and the mainland areas of the West Highlands, dropped by at least half. Several smaller, shorter-lived settlements were also founded on the shores of Loch Resort at this time.

How on earth did such a community survive, and how did it provide for its basic material and social needs?

Two of the five families were of course resident gamekeepers, in full-time employment with the Lewis and Harris estates. They lived in 'white' or slated houses, not 'black' thatched houses. Even so, for Mackenzie of Crola, providing for eight children out of a gamekeeper's wages must have been hard. Kinresort was never a 'typical' crofting community: there is very little cultivable land there. Pastoral agriculture prevailed, and the families each had a couple of cows, as well as sheep, and every family had a boat, for use in a loch teeming with fish. A further source of income was the provision of fresh water to the ships which sheltered in Loch Resort, and while—at least until 1914—there was some kind of commercial fishery in the estuary the inhabitants carried the fish in creels over the moor to Morsgail to add to their income. Kate MacDonald was apparently paid one shilling and sixpence per creel for the ten mile round trip.

Later less arduous employment was available, when Kate was appointed as schoolteacher to her younger brother Murdo. He himself was to become the postman to Ardbheag, another settlement further down the loch, while Malcolm Mackaskill got the job of postman from Kinresort to Morsgail. Undoubtedly such state employment kept the settlement alive.

Did I say less arduous? Murdo MacDonald's round from Crola to Ardbheag involved a five mile walk over rugged country, riven with peat hags and littered with lochans. He was fortunate that, for military purposes during the 1914-18 war, a line of telegraph poles had been erected between Ardbheag and the head of Loch Resort, which he could follow as markers in bad weather. Sadly, these were disconnected on grounds of economy after 1918, and the village lost its only direct link with the outside world. Apparently Lord Leverhulme was approached by the Post Office for a rental to keep the facility open, but Bodach an t-Siabuin (the old soap man, as the detergent magnate was locally known), who had bought the island from the Mathesons, declined. In the absence of a road or communications link, the postmen were the village's life-support system.

Malcolm Mackaskill's round was equally hard. He had to build his own markers—a line of cairns—over the moor to Morsgail to follow in bad weather: apparently he had a dram concealed in one of them for sustenance. But on his return journey he also carried food, clothing, and once the villagers had radios, re-charged batteries on his back, often amounting to a 70 1b. burden. Malcolm was awarded the BEM for his services to the community. He died at the age of 88, so his rigours obviously did him no harm.

But other needs of the community, apart from earning a living, had to be met. The Education Act of 1872 provided the first schoolteacher, Malcolm Macleod, who lodged with his pupils' parents. In 1883 he had eleven pupils at Crola. But with the arrival of the new families at Luachair in 1885, numbers increased and soon there were 25 pupils— including some from Dirisgil, down-loch. A school was needed. A. J. Mackenzie, born in Crola in 1887, describes in his unpublished autobiography what happened.

> Under my father's direction the good folk of Kinresort planned to build a schoolroom with suitable accommodation for the teacher attached. The first task was to collect stones and clay...In a remarkably short time the walls of the clay biggin were up to the necessary height...Every bit of wood used in the building was collected on the shores of Loch Resort and the Ardmore...Benches, forms, doors, windows and furniture were all made by my father...

The school building also served as a meeting-house and church. Regular visits were made by ministers from Uig parish in Lewis and from Harris.

The schoolhouse/church building is still there, though in sad disrepair, with benches broken and the roof rusted away. Its restoration would be a worthy project. In the former teacher's accommodation lies a smashed bakelite radio, for which Malcolm Mackaskill had probably carried in the batteries. I wondered if it had belonged to Murdo MacDonald and his sister Kate, who moved into the empty schoolhouse when their croft across the river became too hard work for Murdo, who was not robust. Kate complained that in her new home she missed the view to Scarp, whence had come her forefathers.

Murdo must have been the last child born in Kinresort, and the only one to be of educable age after 1914. By this time, the school had been closed, and his sister employed to teach him at primary level. Later he taught himself Greek and Latin, and impressed a minister visiting Loch Resort by completing a quotation from Homer that the minister had started, in the original Greek.

He read voraciously: literature, science, religion and politics, borrowing books from passing ships, from John Smith the schoolmaster at

Crowlista who befriended him, and by joining various book clubs, becoming probably the remotest subscriber to the Left Book Club in the 1930s! For Murdo's reading made of him a Christian socialist, and though influenced by Marx, he was probably closer spiritually to Tolstoy, whose tracts he read. He wrote to John Smith, an activist in the Labour Party,

> If communists read the New Testament...they would find that Christianity is the religion of the poor. I am not aware of any tenet or belief in Protestant religion which cannot be reconciled with the economic theory of Communism...

His politics led him to support Malcolm MacMillan's successful campaign to become the Labour MP for the Western Isles in 1935; and his religion, to sit the entrance exams for Glasgow University, where he intended to study divinity: exams he passed with ease. Murdo's education led him into no Celtic twilight, but towards Calvinism and Marxism. His letters to John Smith show no interest in Gaelic culture or history. Indeed he remarked that the election result of 1935 was 'the first time I have ever felt consciously proud of belonging to the Western isles.'

Murdo grew up an isolated, unrobust child, then matured an isolated young man. In a letter to John Smith, he wrote,

> Living here in the back of beyond, the only thing which makes the loneliness bearable, at least to me, is that the door of reading is open to a larger world of fact and imagination.

His infrequent trips to Uig, and even less frequent ones to Stornoway, gave him social contacts, as did the visits to Kinresort from his cousins in the summer months. But a terrible loneliness emerges from his letters. As a grown man he visited Crowlista and sat at the back of the class in school 'just to see what it was like'.

Alas, Murdo was never to take up his University place. As the clouds of war—which as a pacifist he dreaded—broke over Europe, he was afflicted by an illness, possibly a brain tumour, and died, aged 33, in 1940.

Under Murdo's pillow on his death was found a long poem in Gaelic, expressing a Christian resignation towards his approaching death. His library remained in the old school house when his sister left in 1961; so too did an open Bible on the pulpit. The pulpit is now full of sheep fleeces, the Bible and library long gone.

Murdo MacDonald and John MacDonald with his motor bike

Murdo's attitude to his isolated upbringing in Kinresort contrasts markedly with that of A. J. Mackenzie, mentioned earlier, who talks of his boyhood as a magical time:

> We made our own music, and very good music it was. Bagpipes, fiddles, accordions and Jew's harps...our lack of books was in large measure compensated for by gifted old men who could regale us with thrilling tales of days and deeds long past.

Although this is the reminiscence of an old man who left Crola at the age of four (and who was nearly shipwrecked in the 'Zulu' fishing boat that carried the family to Crowlista), and who only re-visited the place once, twenty years later, it does reflect the fact that Mackenzie lived in a bustling village, while Murdo lived in a dying one. Unlike Murdo, Mackenzie qualified for the ministry, following a career in the south as an Army Chaplain.

If Murdo's birth in 1907 was the last in Kinresort, the final marriage appears to have been celebrated in 1916. But on her marriage, the bride, a Morag MacDonald, removed to Bernera, Lewis, with her husband. This woman's daughter, now living in Inverness, told me of a tragic occurrence at the wedding celebration. A young man from Luachair had been sent to Tarbert, Harris, to buy the drink for the wedding. He went missing, and after a search his body was found by Loch Bhoshmid, a place reputedly haunted, where he had died of apparent heart failure. This tale appears to have entered local folklore to such an extent that I have heard three separate variations on the story. In one of them, his name is given as Angus Mackaskill.

The removal of the bride, and death of the young man, seem almost symbolic of the fate of the village which, after 1918, was living on borrowed time. Bold attempts to breach its isolation were made by John MacDonald of Luachair, who acquired a motor bike, which he manfully lifted across moor and river on his trips to Harris. Though resident in Luachair, he was a lay missionary, and carried the word to the needy souls of Harris. But without a road, Kinresort was doomed.

Thus, by 1953, according the the *Stornoway Gazette*, there were only three bachelors and three spinsters in the village, which still had no road, shop, doctor or telephone link to the outside world. Though the paper argued for the construction of a road, it was already too late. Annie Mackaskill, brother of Malcolm, died in 1959. Kate MacDonald (Kate 'Crola') moved out in 1961, and Donald Buchanan, the Harris gamekeeper, in 1963, leaving the settlement deserted. Not even the dead remained, for there was never a graveyard at Kinresort, the deceased being taken back to Scarp for burial.

My interest in Kinresort had been aroused years ago on seeing the black dots on the map, signifying a settlement. But I first managed to visit it in 1991, walking in from Ardbheag by Murdo's postal round, and passing the Dos stone, where Ulla the Beast was slain by Dos Mor Mac A'Cheannaiche—according to *The Traditions of the Western Isles*, collected by the Sgoilear Ban from Dirisgil, further down the loch. One of the stories Mackenzie listened to with rapture, but which held no interest for Murdo? Another time I walked in by Mackaskill's cairns with my son, stopping at the beehive airighs (shielings) at Bheannasgil on the moor. Over these moors, not long ago, was reputed to roam Mac ant-Sronaich, a cannibal who preyed on children tending airighs such as these. Thence we descended the moor to the loch.

And what remains of Kinresort today?

The schoolhouse is disintegrating, the croft houses only bare walls. The better-built gamekeepers' houses still stand. That in Crola is boarded up. The Luachair house is in better condition, and still used for three months in the year by salmon bailiffs, and occasionally shepherds and others. The two bridges between Luachair and Crola are also long gone. So too are the conditions which produced the Murdo MacDonalds of this world, something we may regret, but that he himself would probably have welcomed.

April:
RITES OF SPRING

It is a short time from Easter to May, but the change wrought from relief at mere survival over winter, to the burgeoning of energy and optimism, is enormous. With the cruellest month dying, life stirs in our hearts. We believe again, make plans for ourselves and the mountains. And this was an ambitious and complicated plan.

Davie had, with justification, been complaining. We hardly ever, he pointed out, got above 3,000 ft these days: a Corbetteering coup seemed to have taken place in the group. It was my duty to make amends, as unofficial secretary, treasurer and chairman of the Stobcross Gentlemen's Mountaineering Club. I knew the Monklands Mafiosi were planning to visit Resourie bothy in Ardgour, with plans to ascend all sorts of eminences which I personally would have had little objection to seeing disappear down a Superquarry.

So I presented my plan to Davie. We would go separately, doss Wild Rover fashion somewhere on the Friday night, and cross to Mull next day for Ben More. Then we would get the last ferry and arrive at Resourie for the party. A new peak, a new island: he was convinced. And so was the Lad. So we drove to Corran Ferry in apparently settled weather, but out of which sudden, sharp squalls would be thrown. At Corran we had an appointment in the bar. With the Ladies Lyric Choir Walking Club, with whom this was a joint meet. As secretary, I was justifiably nervous.

'What's all this about lassies then? I suppose that'll be dirty talk barred this trip?' queried the Lad.

I explained that the ladies had often expressed a desire to sample bothying. That they had criticised our male-bonding masculinist approach to the thing, and exclusion of females—which of course I denied, thus feeling bound to invite them and being astonished when they accepted. I did not tell the Lad that if there was any dirty talk, it would probably be from the Ladies Lyric Choir.

We picked the pair of them up, crossed the ferry and headed for Lochaline, their car following ours at a respectful distance. It was so long since I had been there, as a child, that it was new to me. A faery land of wooded hills, deep glens and fingers of loch are the lands of Ardgour and Morven, especially when seen in a magical *abendrot* as they were that evening.

We found there was no ferry waiting room at Lochaline to doss in. We had a tent for three, so tried to find a caravan for the ladies, to no avail. Finally we erected the tent in a muddy field, and vacated the cars to the ladies: they could each have a rear seat and a good kip. But first we would visit that pub on the pier at Lochaline, for one pint.

The place was hoachin. It was like a Glasgow working mens' club: fags, booze and country music. For some reason, many of the inmates were from Glasgow, and the whole place was friendly. So there were pints, and pints. And pints. We had to sign something saying we were members, and then there was more drink, more music. I got in a heated discussion with Davie, and at one point he said,

'Ye're a Frankenstein's Monster. I created ye wi my own hands, and look at ye now!' In the Guinness wisdom I understood, but on sobering lost the meaning. I must ask him again, someday, to explain. But it was late when we bedded, and late when we rose to rush for the early ferry, throwing pans and stoves and food into the back of the car we took across. Breakfast was eaten in the waiting room at Fishnish in primitive conditions. I wondered if the Ladies were enjoying themselves, as I watched the bacon grease harden on their nail varnish.

The mist was down, but the wind rose and lifted it as we drove to Loch na Kael, and by the time we had prepared ourselves it was a clear day with a tugging wind. It was also cold in the wind, and I noticed there was a powdering of new snow, or old ice, on the summits of the hills. But it was sharp, fine, with Coll out to sea beyond Ubha and Gometra, a pallette of green, russet and yellow islands.

The wind strengthened as we ascended the burn to A' Chioch, and it was blowing hard by the time we did the scramble to the top, though luckily it relented as we dropped to the Ben More col. The horizon was ever-retreating before us, revealing more and more, especially out to sea where Rum, Eigg, and the beaches of Coll and Tiree were visible, as well as Jura far to the south. Landward it was more hazy: Knoydart? The Ben? Ben More looked dramatic in the light reflecting off the accumulation of ice-particles the wind had built up along the rocks on the ridge. Many of these broke off and flaked through the air in the wind. One white flake crossing the hill revealed itself as a winter-ermined hare.

The day improved and improved, till we had run out of hill and were descending. We stopped by a burn in the sun, now warm with the wind fallen, and rested. Everyone dozed, tired after the previous night's revels. Then we sauntered further down to the loch, where tourists in their cars were sun-bathing. We found a green sward and joined them, Davie reliving his youth with a 'drum-up' by the loch. One of the Ladies suggested, 'Wouldn't it be better to go to a tea-shop?'—but did not pursue her suggestion beyond Davie's snort of derision. Actually it might have been an idea. It took so long to get a 'bile' that it proved to be a mad rush for the ferry, and then a mad drive to get the last call for pub grub at Strontian, before another drive took us to the road end at Resourie and the most agonising of moral dilemmas—an open, unlocked gate. To drive on, or not to drive on, that was the question. Eventually we decided against taking the chance of having our vehicles impounded, and walked the three miles or so along the track to where the bothy was supposed to be.

Now, none of us had ever been there before, but it was clear from the map: the track virtually went to the doss. So, no problem even in pitch black. (Nights seem to be darker nowadays than they were.) Only, as we were to discover in daylight, a new section of forest had been opened up, and the path by-passed the doss now by quite a bit. But we didn't know that. We came upon a couple of cars, including the Boomerbus, parked by a gate. We examined behind the gate and it appeared to drop vertically into a pathless, Amazonian jungle of rain-forest. Though later to deny it, all initially agreed that that wasn't our route. But after floundering about in cul-de-sacs, or taking the main path ever higher up the hill in the wrong direction, we decided: it must be down there.

Davie and I left the Ladies in the hands of the Lad, and ventured down. At first it was a toboggan-run of slimy mud, then it flattened out to be more like descriptions I had read of Canadian forest, the way leading along breaks floored with rotting vegetation, the danger of leg-snap at every step. We had torches, but it was so dark we could see no sky above the trees. I was just about to call a halt when Davie said, 'I saw a spark'—and disappeared into the darkness. I waited. A few minutes later he returned.

'The torch light hit aff the roof. Go and get the rest o them.'

We collected our companions who slithered, bounced and fell their way to Resourie. One Lady had skid-marks of mud from shoulder to heel, I later noticed. But at first I was too gobsmacked to notice much, as we entered to an amazing scene. There was a huge fire blazing in the hearth, an accordionist giving it laldy to the accompaniment of a guitarist, while Erchie and the Dominie were holding forth with the vocal line. We had a party, we had whisky, so thoughts of bed were brushed aside and forgotten till the hour before the dawn.

The accordionist was the bothy maintenance man, up to repair a door, which he did expertly the next day. He was also an expert musician and gave us a medley of Scottish airs, while Erchie threw in examples from his repertoire of folk songs. I suggested to the Ladies: 'Aye, ye'll nae get this on the Byres Road on a Saturday night!'—and I called on the Lad, 'Gies wan o yer Knickerwetter specials!'

'What's that?' asked the Dominie, showing his interest in comparative ethnology, 'A German folk-song?'

'Na,' I replied, 'Its wan o his songs fae the sixties, that gets the lassies needin a change o underwear.'

His mock reluctance overcome, the Lad grabbed the proferred guitar and gave us all the great Orbison numbers, and a few k.d. lang ones forbye. You could tell by the misty eyes that they were doing their work. In fact, when Erchie sang 'The Bachelor fae Inverness', the most ideologically unsound and politically incorrect song ever written, to quote from which would make me blush, the Ladies yelled for a repeat.

I was shocked, and commented, 'You lassies are a disgrace tae yer sex. I mean you wid probably love the joke aboot the Gorilla and the Nun.'

I had made a mistake. It was more than my life was worth to refuse to tell it. Violence would have resulted. And it was an uproarious success. Davie looked at me and through the laughter he said, more in sorrow than anger, 'It's a terrible indictment o wimmen.'

Then Erchie took over, cleared away the chairs from the flagstone floor and organised the dancing, though due to the sexual imbalance of the company, some men were given the honorary designation of 'quasi-women' by the Boomer. I must confess that I missed the last of the revels. Davie and I mounted the stairs and participated vicariously in the party, with the Dominie soon following, to listen to the hooching and chooching from a horizontal position. When we finally emerged at midday on the Sunday, the Lad had vanished with the Ladies, getting an early lift home, the Mafia were out in a blinding downpour on a Corbett, and the accordionist was sorting the door. We had a Festerday, all day. Watching the rain, drinking tea: blethering. And went home on the Monday.

The lassies never came again. Erchie would ask about them every now and then.

'Nice lassies. And they had a great time in yon bothy. Ye'd hae thought they wid come back. You keepin them tae yersel?'

I was able easily to plead innocent to such a charge, but found it more difficult resolving the Boomer's puzzlement. I tried:

'Maybe, Erchie, it's no whit they found, which they liked. But whit they didnae find, which wis mair important.'

At any rate, that was the one and only S.G.M.C. Dance, our one Rite of Spring.

Echo:
The Pollokshaws Mullach

In August 1920, a small neat man was crossing to Lewis on a MacBrayne's ferry. It is unlikely that any of his fellow passengers knew him, though he was a person both renowned and reviled. Renowned to those like Lenin, the leader of the recently-founded Soviet state, who described him as one of 'the isolated heroes who assumed the heavy task of precursors of the revolution' during World War One. His opposition to that war on socialist grounds had made him reviled by the British government, which repeatedly jailed him during and after the war for his internationalist activities. In one of his defence speeches, in 1915, he had stated, 'I have been enlisted for fifteen years in the socialist army. It is the only army worth fighting for: God damn all other armies.'

What was this man doing on the Cal-Mac ferry to Innsegal? Though he was prematurely aged by his experiences, and weakened by the poverty of unemployment, he was not going on a holiday on that day three quarters of a century ago.

John MacLean was born in Pollokshaws in 1879, of working-class parents who were classic victims of the Highland Clearances. His father, Daniel, had been born on Mull (homeland of the Maclean clan) in 1845, and forced to shift as a youth to Glasgow, where he laboured as a potter in various factories, the work eventually killing him with a form of silicosis in 1887. His mother's parents had been cleared from Corpach, and Anne MacPhee and her mother walked to Glasgow, their new home. Anne became a weaver in a local textile factory. After the Irish, with about fifteen per cent of the population, the Gaels, with about half that, were the biggest 'national minority' in the burgeoning industrial metropolis.

Respectable working-class people, the MacLeans do not appear to have been political, but were good Calvinists who belonged to the original Secession Church. MacLean originally adhered to this Church as well, and even took his teacher-training at the Free Church Training College, but by the turn of the century he had adopted the Marxist view of religion as the 'opium of the people' and by 1903 he had joined the Marxist British Socialist Party.

However, some of his calvinist views fitted in with, or influenced his Marxism, such as his near-messianic view that the revolution was predestined to succeed. His belief in the place of education as the key to working class salvation, and in the role of an elect of educators, echoes traditional Presbyterian thinking. He even looked like a minister! And his morality, teetotalist and driven by a work-ethic which probably helped to kill him, is familiar to many active or lapsed Calvinists.

His more formal Highland links are difficult to establish. It is doubtful if he visited Mull, the land of his ancestors. His pre-war socialist agitation took him to Lerwick a few times, but not, apparently, to the lands of the Gael. While the family tongue was Gaelic, and John doubtless heard it at church, there is no indication that he spoke it. Improvement and respectability for Glasgow Gaels at that time meant English for the children. Nevertheless, he did sign his articles in the B.S.P. paper *Justice* before World War One with the pseudonym 'Gael'. He had heard from his grandmother tales of the wickedness of the Clearances, which later he would find echoed in Marx's *Capital* and articles on the Sutherland Clearances.

Like most Marxists, Maclean had given little thought to the land question before 1918, apart from general comments about the need for scientific, collective agriculture, and the welcoming of the establishment of 'land colonies' of the unemployed. The entire emphasis of people like Maclean was on the struggle of the industrial working class, which they hoped would lead to world socialist revolution. But by 1920 it was clear that such expectations had suffered a set-back.

Emphasis shifted. For Lenin and the Bolsheviks it moved to the 'anti-imperialist' struggles of the colonies for their independence, and Maclean too shifted his focus, believing now that world revolution would come out of the break up of the British Empire, and he moved to support for Scottish and Irish nationalism, causes he had previously opposed. It was this shift that turned his attention towards the Highland land problem, for it brought him into touch with various individuals—like Erskine of Mar—and organisations, like the Highland Land League, which also favoured Scottish independence.

Maclean had participated in Highland Land League meetings, and in August 1920 attended their Annual Conference, supporting resolutions on Scottish independence and public ownership of the land. The conference took place at a time of widespread land seizures in the Highlands, following on the frustrations of demobilised, landless ex-servicemen. Mull itself had been so effectively cleared that there was little place for land agitation. On Lewis, however, where population was highest and with a tradition of land agitation, conditions were, Maclean felt, ripe—and so he took the boat to Stornoway.

The struggle of the Lewis people with Lord Leverhulme for land after 1918 was probably the last major land war in Britain. In the spring of 1920, 29 men seized land and began building houses at Coll, while another 21 did likewise at Gress. These were followed by other raids at Carnish, Reef, Orinsay and elsewhere. The story of these raids has been told by others—notably in Donald MacDonald's *Lewis: a History of the Island*—but Maclean's intervention appears to have been forgotten. At the time however, it certainly was noticed, especially by the *Stornoway Gazette*, which on 13 August 1920 devoted a hostile article—'Bolshevists in Lewis'—to Maclean's activities. Thereafter the *Gazette* continued to attack Maclean and the Land League, which it saw as a Bolshevist conspiracy.

By 1920 Maclean had adopted the view that the old clan system was basically communist, and felt that its communal traditions should be revived on a modern basis. In *Vanguard* he wrote:

> We must encourage the Highlanders to co-operate communally, to culti-
> vate the land with the latest machinery and the latest discoveries of science,
> and to communally catch fish as well...

Maclean visited the land raiders at Coll, but found many of them away at the fishing. He then returned to Stornoway to address a public meeting. Here he had a hostile reception, as many of the town workers blamed the land raiders for the suspension by Leverhulme of schemes which had provided employment. It is also clear that Maclean's stance against the recent war did not endear him to the ex-servicemen in his audience. The *Gazette* commented approvingly, 'His attempt to inculcate the audience with the views of Bolshevism was not so successful as doubtless he had anticipated it would be.'

After his visit, the *Gazette* continued to thunder against Maclean in editorials, announcing 'all Lewismen are loyal to their King and Country…and not of the Bolshevist type', and even publishing poems against him! They also pursued him to Glasgow, where at a Land League meeting they reported Maclean as saying to a more favourable audience:

> Cowardice had come to the Highlands. He did not blame the people. It was their state of dependence on Lord Leverhulme that made them cowards. The same servile spirit that characterised Highland gamekeepers and Highland policemen was at work in Stornoway. (*Stornoway Gazette* 27 August 1920)

Later Maclean showed his bitterness at the land-raiders' compromises when he wrote in November's *Vanguard* that they had sold their sons' lives for a mess of pottage. The Highland land agitation subsided, and so too did Maclean's brief and rather unsuccessful intervention in Highland politics. Like many others, he had gone to the Hebrides convinced he would find something which, in fact, did not exist—in his case, communistically-inclined crofters. He might, however, have seen the spread of Crofters' Trusts three quarters of a century later as a welcome resurgence of the collectivist traditions of the Gael.

Among the high flats of a much-changed Pollokshaws today there is a monument to Maclean, who died there in 1923. It reads:

> Famous pioneer of working class education,
> He forged the Scottish link in the
> Golden Chain of World Socialism

Nearby is the John Maxwell School, where Maclean taught Marxist economics at night-classes before 1914. Today the school houses a bilingual Gaelic primary unit, maintaining the traditions established by Glasgow's Gaels.

May:
BELTANE

It was a dreadful day of rain and wind before we left, and a similar day on the drive back down. But these bracketed two fine days, one of mixed cloud and sun and the other one of the most Alpine days I have seen in Scotland, when there were three colours only: white snow, blue sky, black rock.

Erchie's knee was still giving trouble, but he was plodding on, though taking a rest from driving as I had the wheel and the Lad relieved me occasionally. It is not that I doubt Erchie's driving skills, but I feel better with my hands on the wheel. Erchie's driving is a metaphor for how many people regard life: get past the next obstruction, and the way will be clear. It is pointless to tell Erchie that if the Boomerbus does succeed in overtaking whatever caravan or lorry is in front of it, it will only mean it catches up with the next one, or meets one coming out of a side road. So his driving is sedate, relaxed stretches of 'clear road ahead', punctuated by frenzied white-knuckle interludes of overtaking on narrow Highland roads.

I ignored Erchie's constant back-seat advice on how to outstrip caravans, and the Lad's view that the Lada probably couldn't do it anyway, and carried them all safely to the Big Grand Cluanie Dam. Here we left Erchie to cross the dam and traverse Ben Loyne. Then we would meet him at the pub in Cluanie. He was intending to traverse the mile after mile of Ben Loyne summit bog, which seemed to me strange therapy for a wounded knee. Crossing the Glen Loyne dam was originally his intention: however after trying various Indiana Jones gyrations on that dam which lacks a footpath across, he gave up. I looked at the endless miles of his Corbett, and wished him well.

The Lad and I progressed a little further, aiming for A' Chralaig and Mullach Fraoch-Choire. We headed off up the path in sunshine like silk, and soon cut up over the moor towards our first summit. It was a steep pull over moor, then scree. The sharp cone of Ciste Dubh to our west, changing shape as we rose, gave us pleasant distraction till the summit of A' Chralaig, where we took a wee break and looked around at the endless ranges stretching north, south and west. I said to the Lad,

'I quite envy you, ye know. You still have all this to do, it's all still a mystery to you.'

Before leaving we looked for the sun glinting on Erchie's bauldy heid on Ben Loyne, but failed to see it.

The northern-facing slopes of our hills were still heavily embedded in snow, though it was peeling away from the ground, revealing the largest crevasse formations I had ever seen in Scotland. At the col between the two hills we looked down a fissure in the snow which went at least thirty feet before disappearing in an iceblue haze. From the glens below mist was slowly crawling on its belly uphill, outflanking us, preparing to ambush us. The peaks on all sides vanished in a milky fog as we started to ascend Mullach.

We were heading for the Forcan Ridge next day, and I thought it would give the Lad a wee taster of scrambling if we had a practice on the smashing wee shattered pinnacles of the ridge to the summit of the Mullach. But conditions had made it a little more problematic than I had intended. The plastering of late snow had filled up many of the copious cracks of our line of aiguilles, forcing us to keep to the top, where a narrow path of footprints had already been laid down. There was a little exposure at a couple of points, over brief drops.

'I don't really have a head for heights,' muttered the Lad, 'Is this thing tomorrow like this?'

'No, no, not at all,' I truthfully replied.

About half way along we had one of those coincidences which somehow seem utterly natural on the hills: we met Al and a Pal coming down from the summit. Now I hadn't seen him for a few years, since we were climbing with Davie on the Ben, and on our 'standing room only' meeting space we exchanged chatter and patter. They had had it clear on the summit.

'Come tae the pub later on,' I suggested, 'We are meeting the Boomer there, if he survives his solo ascent o Ben Loyne.'

We hastened on, to beat the cold mist, and soon scrambled up a messy gully to the summit, and over to the cairn. Sadly, now we could see nothing of the lands and the peaks we had witnessed from further off, and it was not long before we were chasing after Al and Pal and back to the col.

As we descended, the mist gave up its guerrilla campaign to spoil our day, and retreated to some undiscovered hideout, leaving the summits lifting their faces to the evening sunshine. The sky turned a glorious red as we regained the car. It would be a fine day for our Ridge tomorrow.

Erchie and Al were already well gone in conviviality, and after eating at the cheery hostelry, we joined them and spent a pleasant evening with other mountaineers and fishermen. When I first met Erchie and Al, the talk was all of north faces and hard routes: fine climbers both. I watched with amusement and amazement as the Boomer waxed eloquent about Ben Loyne and its beauties. But more was to come.

I had followed Al up a couple of Nevis routes: he was so good, so confident, he never bothered with a guide-book, just picked his way. But I could see he was relieved when I told him Davie had 'come out' as a Munroist, for his own confession followed: he too had given up struggling against his repressed Munroism. Then, as if about to show me a dirty postcard, he looked around, produced *A Munroist's Almanac* and asked, 'We want to do the Five Sisters tomorrow. This book says to go up by Glen Licht. Do you think it would be all right to just go up from the road by Cluanie?'

I gasped. Here was a man who had dragged my timid self up the vertical faces of Ben Nevis without a guidebook, now hesitating about a *diretissima* assault on 2,000 ft of easy-angled grass outside. There seemed no appropriate answer but, 'Yes. It's all right that way. No problems.'

At chucking-out time the sober ones took the wheels, and we drove to the Cluanie Dam, where we pitched our tents, prolonging our conversations under a sky full of sparkling stars, below which unseen skeins of geese flew, honking.

Next day's logistics were: Erchie would drop us at the foot of the Forcan: on finishing we would descend to Glen Shiel, where he, with a dodgy knee and no insurance, would have taken my car. He was hoping also to plod up another Corbett beside Shiel Bridge to pass the time while waiting for us. For ours would be quite a long day.

'Careful wi that car, Erchie, ' I cautioned. 'Ye arnae used tae performance vehicles.'

'Will we need the axes?' the Lad asked as Erchie left. I did not need to look up at the Ridge whose outline I had checked coming down from Cluanie, before replying that we would.

As we crossed to pick up the stalkers' path, a group of young men with female companions sped past us, yomping like it was their last chance to get some fugitive Argie. As we watched them putting space between them and ourselves, the Lad observed, 'Must be great to be young and fit like that.'

I said nothing, needing my breath for the steepish ascent. But we passed them soon, exhausted and gulping gallons of water from a burn. And another large party of young whippersnappers at Biod an Fhithich, all looking much more like Stallone than we did, and all much more updated in their gear. And again at Meallan Odhar. They seemed to be dropping off like flies, despite the absolutely unsurpassable day of windless sunshine. The route took us eight hours, and I kept looking back at those behind us, who were getting further behind. Now, I think my non-competitive post-macho credentials are as good as any man's. But that pleased me no end—and the Lad too I think. But we tend to be confident enough in our masculinity not to need to mention these things.

Confidence can wilt. When the Lad got a clear view of the Forcan Ridge, foreshortened and steepened as I knew it to be, but still magnificent, the best thing for many miles in any direction, he hesitated.

'We're not going up there, are we?'

'Oh aye we are,' I replied.

I did not mention to him that someone had recently been killed on it, after falling several hundred feet. That might have spoiled his enjoyment. I did tell him, as we went, of the time Davie and I had done the Ridge in a near-hurricane, and covered most of the ground on our knees to the top, so he might appreciate how lucky he was in having such a day for it. Though I noticed the Lad himself did not have much to say, after we set foot and axe on the initial part of the ridge.

There was old ice and recent snow on the ridge, not the best combination. But the rocks, where they showed through, were dry and sound, and we progressed fairly rapidly up the easier, lower part, to where it steepens below Sgurr na Forcan. The Lad had gone totally quiet by now, and I respected the silence all around us to the extent of only giving one piece of advice before we proceeded:

'Don't look doon.'

Though he would occasionally clutch the rock in a passionate embrace, or try to skewer himself with his axe, the Lad really made short work of this final section, and at the top was rejoicing in a widening of his mountain experience. But ahead, I noticed that the ridge to the Saddle itself was heavily corniced, below narrow snow ridges which the wind had raised and sharpened to knife-edges. There was little avalanche debris, but that might just mean it was waiting to go. Waiting for us.

No point in upsetting people, so I did not confide my concerns to the Lad, exulting in the fullness of his manhood behind me, but moved ahead onto the *arête* gingerly. It was rock-solid, and on it a fine firm runnel of steps had already been trodden. No problem, and we were

Descending from the Saddle, with Forcan Ridge in the background

soon at the Saddle summit, sharing it with a young English couple, lad and lass, taking a long spring walking holiday in Scotland. They too were exhilarated, and I, a little carried away, put forward the view that it was just like a day in the Alps.

'Yes, but in the Alps you never get the variation in the sky, in the cloud, like you do in Scotland, and then there's the colours of the moor here, the sea below…'

I looked at him, thinking: you can come back, pal, if ever we get round to handing out permits to your compatriots at the border. But did not say it, for the English are usually deficient in a sense of irony, take everything literally.

We pressed on, many miles still to go over the subsidiary summits of the Saddle, where we had good sport on the frozen snow ridges, and fine views into dark, secret corries, before we picked up a stalking path which zig-zagged down to Coire Uanie, and thence to Shiel Bridge. It was a puggled duo who arrived to find the Boomer in the Lada, enjoying his pre-prandial can of lager in the soft sunshine. We bartered it off him, with the promise of replacing it with double quantities in the pub, but even then he seemed miffed at being disturbed at his imbibing. Later we replaced lost bodily tissue and eased bodily aches and pains with food and drink. But it was a peerless May Day evening, too good to spend in the pub.

'We've had a Solstice fire at Midsummer: let's hae a Beltane fire on May Day,' I suggested. The Boomer agreed, pointing out that there were limitless supplies of driftwood at the Cluanie Dam. Soon we were in the car, and away. I tried to remember. Solstice fires I was all right on, but Beltane ones? Was it not something to do with chasing away evil spirits? Aye, that would do for an alibi.

When the level of the loch at Cluanie was raised, it submerged several standings of pinewoods and birch, which were eventually loosened, uprooted and then bleached by the waters. By the loch we found an elephants' graveyard of wood, heapings of tusks and ribs, honed down by water to a bone-like smoothness. A charnel-house of fuel. Many were delicately coloured in browns and greys, polished like pebbles on a beach. Others assumed fantastic shapes, such as the antlers of a moose, or the jawbones of a whale. It seemed a shame, almost, to burn them.

We took a big load, but the fire consumed them quickly as we lay outside by the tent in the firelight, drinking and reliving the fine day we had just had, for Erchie too had climbed his Corbett and explored new country, enjoying it as much, though in a different way, as the Lad had his expedition on Forcan Ridge and the Saddle.

'Gie's the Big Grand Cluanie Dam, Erchie,' I suggested, 'yon Lonnie Donegan wan.'

Erchie sung to us, but we were tired and fell asleep. Then he sang for a while to himself, and on waking and turning, I heard him singing quietly in the snap and sift of the flames. Eventually we fought the few yards to the tent and bed, but Erchie stayed up till he had burned the wood and the fire had gone out. Singing. In the morning the embers were still warm. He had stayed up a long time, warding off the evil spirits.

But as we decamped the rain came on, and pocked the ashes with its drops, raising a little cloud from the now-dead dust and charred stubs. It rained most of the way homewards.

Echo:
West Affric: Saints and Sinners

From the top of Mullach we had looked down into the depths of West Affric, but were unable to see anything for the mist. The fine peaks flanking the glen were invisible. Invisible too were the marks of human passage, and in this section I would like to take you below the mist and let you hear some of the echoes from the history of the glen, especially its more recent history.

Traces of human usage predate even the rickles of undressed stone— old shielings which have left no record of their inhabitants. Upper Glen Affric has many such ruins from pre-Clearance times, when the inhabitants were mainly of the Chisholm clan. Other traces are those on the map, place-names which indicate former human passage. One such, at the west end of Loch Affric, is Athnamulloch (sometimes given as Altnamulloch)—the ford of the Mull men—where tradition relates a band of island caterans were repelled at the river crossing. There certainly was a skirmish here later. In 1721, Commissioners trying to collect rents from forfeit Jacobite estates were confronted by 300 armed men, and retreated after some bloodshed. The Young Pretender himself passed by Athnamulloch on his flight after Culloden, but left no 'Prince's Stone' or 'Prince's Cave' in the glen, though it is possible he climbed

A'Chralaig, becoming thus an early Munro-bagger!

The earliest echo given by the map relates to St Duthac, Irish saint and missionary from the eleventh century, who traversed the upper glen en route from Ireland to his church in Tain. The western exit from Affric to Kintail was known locally as the Cadha Dhuich, St Duthac's Pass, and near the top is a well, Topar Dhuich, bearing the saint's name. Other echoes are so faint we cannot distinguish them: what happened on or near the innocuous-looking Sgurr Gaorsaic (Peak of the Horror), to give it its name?

After missionaries and armed bands, the glen was used as transit for commercial purposes. Though it was never one of the main routes, cattle drovers used the east-west line of the glen for taking beasts to Beauly, or contoured the shoulder of Ciste Dubh, to link up with one of the main cattle-droving roads which went south via Cluanie. One of their resting places was the lonely cottage of Camban. This was occupied by a shepherd, Morrison, as early as 1839, at a time when the whole area was under sheep. Sheep gradually gave way to more lucrative deer, and by the 1890s there was a stalker in Camban. Its last occupants—who left in 1920—were the family of the stalker Paterson. We are lucky enough to have an account of a walker's reception at Camban in 1905. The Rev. R.M. Cairney wrote in the *Cairngorm Club Journal* as follows:

> We pushed [on] and made for Camban, where we got a right royal reception. Our host had spied us on the way a mile or two before and calmly waited our approach at the east foot of Bhein Fhada. The strains of the pibroch greeted us while yet half a mile from the cottage...Our hostess had a huge supper of porridge and thick cream ready for us on the table before we had got the bog wiped from our clothes.

Camban was at a good piece of ground, and an old photo shows tended agricultural land and outbuildings, traces of which can still be clearly seen in ruined dykes. The walker Ben Humble passed by Camban in the mid 1930s, when it was deserted, and noted that names scrawled on walls indicated people were 'dossing' in the house. Today it has been restored as a bothy by the Mountain Bothies Association. But expect nothing more than four walls and a roof!

The longest-inhabited building in the West Affric estate is undoubtedly Alltbeithe, a couple of miles east of Camban. This was occupied from at least 1842, when Morrison moved from Camban to stay at Alltbeithe for 25 years as a shepherd. The original habitation, marked on the O.S. 1880 map, was the stone ruin across the burn from the present wood and corrugated-iron structure, built in 1912. Today it serves as the remotest hostel in the SYHA chain, but its traditions of hospitality stretch back much further. Although briefly occupied by another keeper after they left in 1942, Alltbeithe's last long-term occupants were the Hendersons, who arrived there in 1925. They had a family of five children, and a resident schoolteacher. Both Ben Humble and Tom Weir mention being given food and drink by the welcoming Hendersons as they passed the cottage. Their hospitality went further, and they continued the tradition of giving shelter to mountaineers, in the absence of alternatives in such a remote area.

One of the teachers who boarded with them was a Kirsty Mackay from South Uist. She recorded her own welcome, with a glass of whisky, after arriving by boat and horse from Affric Lodge in 1936. Climbers and walkers were welcome too, and she tells how they were put up in the byre by the Hendersons. I myself once met, in the present hostel, an Italian who was following his father's pre-war trek to Kintail; the latter had been given shelter in Alltbeithe. The Hendersons must have welcomed the company of passing walkers in their isolated home. But if the weather was fine, they would walk nine miles to Affric Lodge for a lift to church at Cannich, in the gamekeeper's car. (Kirsty recalls her memories, in Gaelic, in *Gairm*, No 136.)

Earlier writers extol the hospitality of Alltbeithe as well. In 1912 a W.A.Brigg wrote in the *Scottish Mountaineering Club Journal* (where he also noted that Camban was still occupied) of the Hendersons' predecessors, the Scotts, who came in 1875 and left in 1919:

> At Alltbeithe, a stalking lodge in Glen Affric, we were warmly welcomed by the keeper Mr Scott and his wife, a Harris woman…They had no meat or bread, but with scones and eggs and marmalade we were made happy, and a nine hour sleep rounded off a good day.

Previously, in 1898, the Rev. A. E. Robertson had been similarly entertained with Mrs Scott's tea and scones and noted that she (whom he described as a 'Shetland woman') was busily occupied sorting and carding wool. Thus the Alltbeithe occupants had sheep, as well as cows for milk and chickens for eggs. With seven children as well, Mrs Scott was a busy woman!

But though Alltbeithe may have had hens and some sheep, it was not a croft, but a stalker's house, and occasionally this led to problems, as one W. H. Porter-Fausset found when he tried to go walking in the stalking season in 1909, and discovered Mrs Scott a different woman then! He was so outraged at his treatment that he wrote to the *Daily*

News, who published his letter in November 1909. Let us give him the floor. It is September...

> It was getting dark and raining. A woman opened the door to us and we asked if she would give us a shake-down for the night...saying we should be glad to pay her for her trouble. She refused point-blank, on the grounds that 'the gentlemen who took the shooting would not like it, and her husband would lose his job as under gamekeeper.' We pointed out that we might come to serious harm. 'Surely the gentlemen would not like that?' 'Indeed,' said she, 'what would they care?'
>
> The nearest accommodation was twenty miles away, and I asked to see her husband. He...agreed to give us shelter, on condition that we left at daybreak and went straight back to Cluanie, leaving the mountains alone. We had perforce to accept these conditions.

At this time the Earl of Durham 'took the shootings', and it was common practice to forbid the giving of accommodation to hillwalkers. In this he was not alone. A previous tenant of Affric estate was the American Walter Winans. This man took virtually all the shooting from Cluanie to Achnasheen, and from Kintail to Cannich, as well as some in Atholl! His aim, for which other 'sportsmen' and ghillies disapproved of him, was to massacre as many beasts in as small a time as possible. Thus all disturbances which might diminish his 'bag' had to be avoided.

Winans had a watchers' bothy built on Mam Sodhail, one of the highest of the hills in upper Glen Affric, complete with fireplace and cooking equipment, and supplied with coal by pony. Here a watcher lived for several months each season: but looking for deer was not his only task. Ensuring all walkers kept to strictly designated rights of way was the other. On one occasion Sir Hugh Munro was followed for miles till he left the estate, by a ghillie checking that he did not leave the path! Used for over thirty years, this bothy fell ruinous by 1905, and the keepers were relieved of an uncomfortable and lonely sojourn lying in ambush for rights-of-way sinners.

Alltbeithe became a youth hostel in 1950. The retired stalker at Glen Affric, Duncan MacLennan, told me how he took the beds for the hostel to Alltbeithe in 1950, with a horse and cart, for the road was still in good condition then. Duncan, in his eighties and retired in Cannich, has a wealth of information about the old times in the glen, and is working on an account of his life there.

It is not often a success story can be related, but here is one. Threats to the use of the hostel, and access, have been removed by the purchase of West Affric by the National Trust for Scotland. The NTS has announced its intention to co-operate with the charity, Trees for Life, in the re-afforestation of an area reduced, by centuries of land misuse, to a virtual desert. The whole estate boasts *one* Scots Pine. Visionary ideas for the re-introduction of lynx, wolf and bear have been mooted.

Progress is already evident. On a recent visit I found that Coulavie at the eastern edge of West Affric had been restored, even sporting curtains! An improvement on how it was described to one traveller in 1856, as 'a very poor place [where] we would get nothing but cakes and whisky', which dissuaded him from visiting it. Today, by the bridge which has replaced the ford of the Mull men, it offers—I was told by the Hostel Warden—accommodation for volunteers working with the Trust and the Trees for Life organisation on fencing, planting and other environmental works between here and Camban. Coulavie was probably a shepherd's cottage before evacuation. It later became a school for the family of Chisholms at Athnamulloch, and eventually a ghillies' bothy between the wars, before falling into ruin.

This estate has in the past echoed to the sound of battle, to the hooves of cattle, and the pibroch of isolated shepherds. Today it offers—at Coulavie, Alltbeithe and Camban—shelter for ecological work parties, hostellers from round the world walking to Kintail, and bothiers roughing it below the wild peaks of Beinn Fhada and Ciste Dubh. Hopefully at least some of these will enrich their enjoyment of West Affric, and the guaranteed rights of access and accommodation they enjoy, by thinking a little about those who were there before them. They may feel themselves echoing the wonder of Kirsty Mackay from Uist, when she opened her eyes on her first morning there,

M'am choinneamh bha' Bheinn Fhada
...Le cleoca teann de schneachda
Air a phasgadh mu a guaillean.

In front of me was Bheinn Fhada
...With a heavy cloak of snow
Draped about its shoulders.

June:
SOLSTICE HIGH-ROUTE

I don't belong to the Greta Garbo school of mountaineering, don't see it as a pursuit of solitude but as a search for community. Mae West's 'come up and see me sometime' appeals more to me. Sometimes, however, it is good to go it alone, go at your own pace, go where you want without compromises. Cut across the lie of the land. A few years ago I felt like that, after a series of highly successful and enjoyable collective mountain experiences. I looked for inspiration, an idea. Found one.

Many long-distance treks in the Western Highlands follow natural glen routes east to west. By breaking across this from north to south, I made myself a journey beyond Glen Affric into the less well-known country beyond.

The region between Cluanie and Achnasheen consists of several hundred square miles of country, devoid, except for its fringes, of permanent human habitation. It contains many fine, though easy, peaks which are amongst the remotest in the country. These merit more than a simple marathon walk to bag in a day, and should be savoured on long cross-country tramps. May is the finest time for the area, when the days are long, midge-free and there are still patches of snow amidst the colour of the new vegetation growth. However, the start to my trip appeared inauspicious. It wasn't May, but June, for a start...

The rain lashed down as I got off the bus at Cluanie Inn, reluctant to proceed. But as it was only 10 o'clock and the pub wasn't open, I shouldered my pack and headed for the Glen Affric track, east of the Inn. At first the going was good, but the track soon became a squelching bog. As the rain was easing off and the tops clearing, I decided to head for the col before Mullach Fraoch-Choire and easier underfoot going. Toiling up the slopes was easier than toiling through the bog.

As the weather got better, the adrenalin ran and despite the pack I gained the col quickly. Soon I was enjoying the narrow ridge of the hill, and a pleasant scramble round a series of easy rocky towers to the summit. Fortune had favoured, if not the brave, at least the obstinate, I thought, as I looked down, in a rapidly-improving afternoon, to the wilds of Glen Affric below my feet, and the Alltbeithe Youth Hostel I was headed for.

The weather was getting better all the time, but the drop to the hostel at Alltbeithe seemed interminable. The building had been one of the first Youth Hostels in Scotland, although on this visit it was showing its age and was in need of repair. With a secure lease from the National Trust for Scotland, the SYHA will hopefully carry this out. There was a bustle about the place as I arrived, and the hostel was almost full—of Germans as I discovered, mainly doing the Cannich-Kintail walk, and all wonderstruck with the beauty and wildness of Glen Affric.

In the evening, round the cosy fire I had often warmed myself at, I decided, as the token Scotsman, to ask the Germans a question. I had been puzzled last summer to meet dozens of them walking from Dalwhinnie to Fort William, and now here they were again.

'Is there a book?' I asked, 'A German guide-book?'

Sure enough, every one of them produced their identical Führer, the guide to off-road walks in Scotland, making them the most adventurous of foreign visitors to our land. The warden told me about seventy five per cent of his bed-nights were Germans, and they kept the hostel solvent. But their adventurousness was limited. Only one or two tried climbing the hills, and these had given up because it wasn't in their Führer.

The next morning I was impatient to set off northwards into country new to me. From the hostel the ascent of Sgurr nan Ceathreamhnan is a short and pleasant one, even with a pack, for a good path goes up the Allt na Faing burn, to gain a ridge which leads easily to the top. From the summit the reason for its name (Hill of the Quarters) is apparent, as it radiates off in four ridges; along one of these I proceeded in the coolish, cloudy day, reaching Mullach na Dheiragain in an hour or so. The vast empty wilderness from Loch Mullardoch to Monar lay ahead of me: and so did a problem. I had nowhere to spend the night.

Like many other walkers I had been inspired when young by reading Stevenson's *Travels with a Donkey*, especially the chapter 'A Night Among the Pines'. Remember it?

Night is a dead monotonous period under a roof: but in the open world it passes lightly, with its stars and dews and perfumes, and the hours are marked by changes in the face of Nature.

Now, I had bothied, hostelled, camped, even spent nights in railway huts, telephone boxes and public toilets, but I had never bivvied before. And I had come prepared—though hoping that the dots on the map at the west end of Loch Mullardoch might afford shelter. Maybe I am agoraphobic, I thought, as I descended Coire Aird to the loch, where I found that a couple of rusted roofs of animal shelters were all that remained. It was early, so I cooked a meal by the loch, then walked on, putting off the dreaded moment when my agoraphobia would be tested. Finally, at the petering out of a path up Coire na Breabaig, I lay down to rest, sipping my hip-flask of whisky. Hoping for a night's deep sleep and Midsummer Dreaming.

I looked around me. Below, to the east, was upper Glen Cannich, where the hydro works had raised Lochs Lungard and Mullardoch, and joined them, flooding several houses. To the west, at the Atlantic/North Sea watershed, the path began to drop to Glen Elchaig, where much more recent evacuations had taken place. I had walked there not long before, finding that at Carnach and Killilan were many recently-vacated, still good dwellings. The estate's owner had bought the place for hunting. He was the Defence Minister of a Gulf state, who came to Scotland maybe once a year. According to the *West Highland Free Press,* 'there was growing disquiet locally over suggestions the sheikh was hastening depopulation of Killilan by demolishing houses and other buildings, and—as one local put it—"making it into a desert".' Kintail always had a reputation for lawlessness, for banditry, and sure enough, one of the Sheikh's boats was burned. The local police in consequence mounted an operation as massive as our government had just done to keep Saddam Hussein's hands off the oil of the Gulf. As a result, two local men were jailed.

My soft bed and the balm of the whisky soon had me dozing. But not for long. I opened my eyes and two huge yellow dragonflies were hovering above me in the half-light: were they carnivorous? Full darkness fell and a little sleep came, but dawn brought me awake at five a.m. Just as I contemplated rising I heard a crow caw out, and saw it surrounded by three buzzards, slowly circling it into a trap by feinting at it when it tried to escape. Then in a swoop and clutch, one of the buzzards grabbed it and they flew off with their still squawking prey. I felt Stevenson's point been made for him.

I breakfasted early, and by seven had ascended the shoulder of An Socach (whence I watched cigar-shaped clouds impaled on the peaks of the Cuillin of Skye) to its summit above wild Coire Mhaim falling away to Loch Mullardoch. Then I made my way down tussocky slopes to join the good track which drops down Allt Coire nan Each to An Gead Loch. This was an old drove road and coffin track from Kintail to the east. The last coffins to be carried on it were those of Alistair MacRae and his wife, who came from Kintail to set up an illicit still at Monar. Here they got squatters' rights by building a house on an island in the loch. Their son Hamish Dhu carried on the business after Alistair's death, until 1900, when he turned in his own equipment to the gaugers (excisemen) for the reward! He was certainly the last illicit distiller on a large scale. The local lairds turned a blind eye to his doings, and the folk of Strathfarrar would delay the gaugers heading for Monar while sending warnings to the MacRaes. Hamish and his sister Mairi were also buried in Kintail. Monar was flooded in 1959, and their house— and others—around Loch Monar shore were burned and then flooded.

I crossed the river above Pait Lodge, and began heading up the endless slopes of Meall Mhor, looking around on the way. Somewhere on the huge, featureless slopes of Meall Mhor were the distilling bothies of Alistair and Hamish. They distilled in winter, often waiting for the snow to melt to cover their tracks, and sold their hooch in the summer at marts and fairs in Beauly and elsewhere. The gaugers never found the bothies, and nor did I, but passed on to the delightful ridge of Lurg Mhor and eventually Bidean a Coire Sheasgaich. It was a fine, though hazy, day and a panorama of peaks mingled with the clouds west to the Cuillin and north to Wester Ross. I was tired. It had been a big day after little sleep. My only thought was to reach Bernais Bothy, which was gained by crossing some rough moorland and a river that could be tricky in spate. The bothy had been renovated in memory of Eric Beard (Beardie) who in his day had held various mountain running records, including that of the Cuillin Traverse. Inside the bothy is a modest memorial to him.

Now I was back on familiar ground, for I had been to Bernais before, with the Monklanders and my boy on his first bothy trip away with the 'Big Boys'. As I approached it I recalled his damming of rivers and building of dykes to protect rowan saplings, and his magical first bothy party, when he sat open eyed and mouthed at Erchie's firelighting and singing skills. Then his walk in from Lochcarron on a scorching day with his first real pack. And suddenly, though I knew I would enjoy my quiet solitude that night, I also wanted to talk to someone other than myself again. I had encountered no one since Alltbeithe, bar the spirits of Hamish MacRae and Beardie. A couple of days in the wilderness was fine, but I would not fancy forty days and nights.

Outside the bothy a few trees had taken root in the ruined byre, showing that even without help nature will recover—if we let her. I built up the wall to help keep the deer out.

Hamish Dhu, poacher and distiller, and his sister

The bothy was empty, and I foraged for a little wood and drank my reserves of whisky by the flames, wondering if the original occupant had obtained his supplies from the MacRaes over the mountain. In the morning it was fine and the Bealach Bernais beckoned, but so did comfort, and instead I crossed over by Corrie Leiridh—a wee Khyber pass—on a good path (which however I lost in forestry workings by the river) to Achnashellach and the train back to civilisation.

The conquest of agoraphobia was one of the lesser things that marked this down as a good trip. Five peaks and footsteps in history were others. And confirmation of the Mae West principle. And the idea that maybe that walk through from Elchaig to Cannich might be interesting...at any rate, it would not be in any Führerbuch.

Echo:
The Drowned World of Mullardoch

Glen Cannich, and its head around Loch Mullardoch, has always been the Cinderella of the three glens which draw off from Strath Glass. While many stories of its beautiful sisters, Glen Affric to the south and Strathfarrar to the north, have been told, and the National Trust and Scottish Natural Heritage respectively manage sections of those, upper Glen Cannich remains something of a *terra incognita*.

The reason is simple: Mullardoch is a drowned world, with the former habitations and tracks of the area being under the combined waters of the (now joined) Lochs Lungard and Mullardoch. It is today a desperately hard task to walk the upper glen. The magnificent hills of the area, such as Sgurr na Lapaich and Beinn Fhionnlaidh, are often approached from neighbouring glens, not from Mullardoch itself. This chapter will give a few glimpses of the lost, underwater world of Mullardoch.

Formerly a very good right of way and minor drove road went up from Strath Glass, along the length of Loch Mullardoch, crossing the watershed of the North Sea and Atlantic, before dropping to Kintail by Carnach and Glen Elchaig. In the late nineteenth century, a horse and cart was sent once a week from the Hotel in Cannich to Beinn

Fhionnlaidh (Ben Ula) Lodge. And the road, though a private one, was good enough to take motor transport as late as the 1940s as far as the lodge. Tom Weir got there in the 1930s by post-bus. After World War Two, when the glen was flooded, the new Hydro Board promised to replace the existing Rights of Way, as it was legally liable to do. Dilatoriness on the part of the Board caused the Rights of Way Society to decide to 'write to the Hydro Electric Board, and remind them of their undertaking to construct new paths where necessary, and in particular to make a new track alongside Loch Mullardoch'.

This was in 1951, and today, little short of half a century later, we are still waiting!

And the raising of the waters flooded not only roads, but homes. Although there are pre-Clearance remains in the glen, the most westerly inhabited house in recent times was at Lungard, at first a shepherd's cottage, then a keeper's. In 1856 it had visitors. Charles Simpson Inglis, with a couple of friends, walked from the Caledonian Canal to Skye in these pre-car, pre-railway days, and he wrote of his experiences in *A Pedestrian Excursion in the Highlands*. They had got lost on Mam Sodhail in Glen Affric, and finally stumbled on Lungard in the dead of night, 'by the merest accident' as Inglis says. As he was feeling along the walls for a door,'That's the wrang gate: gang roon the ither side' said a voice— for the occupant was not a Highlander, but a Teviotdale shepherd, Mr Sword, and his family, brought in to look after the sheep. Inglis describes the rest of the scene:

> The gudewife and the whole family were roused, sheep dogs included...the fire was kindled afresh: the kettle hung on the crook and the gudewife got out a large dish of curds and cream to 'keep us going until the tea would be ready'.
>
> After tea we retired to rest, and they gave us their own sleeping room, a homely but clean apartment.

A writer mentioned in 1941 that Lungard was 'deserted'. Its last occupants were a family of Chisholms, who had also occupied Athnamullach in Glen Affric. These glens were so little frequented in the 1930s that Mrs Chisholm recalled they might go six weeks without seeing another living soul.

Inglis must have been the first pedestrian to visit Mullardoch for pleasure, but as mountaineering became more popular, others followed in his wake. As deer-stalking also increased in popularity, Beinn Fhionnlaidh Lodge was built, with a keeper's cottage at Coire na

Cuillean, a couple of miles east of Lungard. Again, we are lucky enough to have an account of a visit there almost a century ago. The Rev. A. E. Robertson was in the process of bagging all his Munros and stayed in 1899 with the keeper, with whom he climbed Bein Fhionnlaidh and Mam Sodhail. A.E.R. described the keeper—Finlayson—as follows:

> He is quite a young fellow—say 24—but one of the best of his kind I have ever met. So intelligent, so eager for knowledge. He is not married but has a fine old housekeeper, who has not 'the English', or at least very little...He has got a fine wee house, all beautifully lined with wood inside and 'dry as a cork' to use his own expression. He came here from Camban [in Glen Affric]. He is a great reader and the books he has astonishes me. Travel books of all sorts, about fifty of them.

Robertson was the first to finish his Munros, and it is fitting that the second man to do so, the Rev. Burn, stayed several times at another keeper's cottage near Beinn Fhionnlaidh Lodge, Luib na Daimh, while 'bagging' himself, about twenty years later. Burn writes:

> After renewing acquaintance with the genial keeper and his wife, (and their excellent milk and oatcakes), I felt fortified with the remark that, if ever I were out of a job I should become a shepherd or keeper, 'for your heart is in the hills'.

Beinn Fhionnlaidh gets its name from an early inhabitant of the glen, Black Findlay of the Stags, who was a keeper and watcher for Mackenzie of Kintail. Findlay reputedly met a poacher on the hill, and shot him with his bow and arrow!

The glen produced its share of colourful characters. One well known worthy was Coinneach an Airidh, Kenneth of the Shieling, born around 1800. He lived at Luib nam Meann opposite Cosag Cottage on Mullardoch. Coinneach was a poacher, distiller and tall-tale teller. He was a famous marksman. One day he had run out of shot when he saw a deer. He loaded his gun with peas, and next year recognised the deer by the peas growing in its ears. He claimed that the fairies knew of his shooting prowess, and when they saw him would run away saying, 'There's Coinneach with his gun, and he will be shooting a sixpence at us' (the only way to harm them). On another occasion he averred that he had rolled a snowball downhill, which, after gathering up deer and rabbits as it rolled, stopped at his house and provided him with frozen meat for the winter! Coinneach was welcome at every table in the glen, for his entertainment value. He reputedly had a son living in Glen Shiel early this century: another died by falling down a well, when carrying barley on a dark night for the 'bree'.

And the twentieth century has had its characters too. In his book *Isolation Shepherd* Iain Thomson talks about a shepherd called Dolian (Donald Iain) at Mullardoch after the flooding. On one occasion he was handling a difficult area of navigation, at the junction of the two former lochs, when his employer asked him if the water was deep enough. Just as Dolian had assured him, 'Sir, it's as deep as the Pacific', the boat ran aground, almost precipitating its occupants into the loch. Dolian jumped overboard to push the boat off, and was left high and dry—and unable to swim—on the submerged peat hag.

Dolian's bothy was a Nissen hut near to where Beinn Fhionnlaidh Lodge had been. Here on one occasion Thomson found him regaling a party of English walkers with stories, songs, cups of tea and venison chops, and an impromptu recital on his pipes, including 'Scotland the Brave'. The party continued into the night, but the hikers' stamina gave out, and they went to bed in their nearby tent.

We can read of former travellers in the glen, but we cannot see it as they did. W.H. Murray camped near Cosac just after the war, and wrote of a place where he camped, soon to be flooded:

> We re-entered woodland...countless lizards idled on the road. A big carpet of grass lay between a wooded knoll and a shingly beach...

But the woods are gone, the grass and the shingle are gone, as are the fine old stalkers' paths and the habitations of those who occupied the glen. In return, we have inexhaustible sources of non-polluting electricity, which was some compensation, till it was privatised.

A MOVABLE FEAST

'It's nae like him,' I suggested to Davie as we drove north in a huge summer downpour. 'I mean, leavin it tae chance like that.'

Davie was driving us to Poolewe, looking hopefully now and again at the sky for a sign of a break in the weather. But it had been a bad summer and we had little hope. I was puzzling at the behaviour of the Dominie. Here we had a man meticulous and cautious to a fault: not your normal view of a risk taker. In addition he was the possessor of a huge moral reputation. So why had he done it? Risked his spotless honour?

At that very moment (I was explaining to Davie), a ship bearing a work in the name of the Dominie was about to dock. In a few days the work, stating that the said George Washington of Monklands had 'completed his Munros' would be in the shops. Yet there was a Maiden waiting for him in the depths of Carnmore, who had not yet—how shall we put it?—had a toe-job from the Dominie.

'He expected tae be finished,' I added, 'but got held back. He's been rinnin aboot daft for months tryin tae catch up. Erchie has been living like a king as the Dominie had pyed hunners o pounds hirin boats tae Knoydart and up Mullardoch. So there's jist A' Mhaighdean left. Bit if he fails on this trip for some reason...'

The thought of even speaking a stain not yet spotted on the character of the Dominie was so awesome that my voice fell away and I gestured vaguely with my hands. Davie had, as often, a more pragmatic point to make about this mad rush to Carnmore to save the honour of the Dominie.

'Whit a bloody place tae finish! I mean, ye should choose a nice wee thing by the road, rin up and doon it, and then intae the boozers. We'll no even get a pint aff him here.'

'Weel, Davie, in the nature o things, Compleation is a Movable Feast,' I pleaded in mitigation.

So we had a few pints with our supper in Poolewe, waiting for a lull in the rain before we left. There was a consolation for us in all this selfless devotion to a friend. Neither of us had been to Carnmore before, though we had looked down on it, silent, from many a peak in that far Darien of the north-west: from Slioch, from Ben Lair or from Ruadh Stac Mor. A little piece of the great jigsaw we could put into place together for once. It was ten miles, and hard ones at that, I knew. And I donned a heavy pack, full of gear for Skye where Davie and I intended to go after Carnmore. The unrelenting rain made us foolishly reluctant to unpack the excess—which I carried in and out. On any other walk it might have made me weep, as might the new boots which, not broken in, gave me bastinado most of the way. But not on this one.

Three miles or so of lovely riverscape, with trees and cliffs opposite, took us to a deserted Kernsary. After that the remaining distance to Carnmore was fairly equally divided between the worst mire of a track I have ever trodden, a perfect Ypres without the duckboards, and a good stalker's path. We toiled uphill over the moor, which then breasted the brae, and before us was a view that held us in silent exchanges of looks, understanding without speaking. It was a wondrous Horatio MacCulloch painting come alive, with moving clouds and rain, and boiling rivers: the Fionn Loch was before us, with Ben Lair and A' Mhaighdean framing it behind. We lost the path at a river crossing and toiled over open moor. The rain beat sadistically on us. I was so tired by the time I reached the causeway to Carnmore I sat down and almost fell asleep. But it did not matter. This was the most awesome, the most magical mountain landscape I had seen, improved, not faulted, by the conditions. In your mountain life, as in your life in general, there are only a few 'moments in and out of time', to use Eliot's words. Falling in and out of sleep at the causeway was one such moment for me.

Too tired to sleep I lay in the bothy, listening to the rain on the corrugated-iron roof. Finally with dawn I fell asleep soundly, and was roused at midday by the arrival of the Dominie and Erchie (who had spent the night in the Boomerbus at the road-end). There had been no reason to get up earlier. The weather was awful, the hills invisible. And the bothy was a functional shelter and little else: cold, dirty and without a fire. I wondered how the Dominie's resolve would deal with the situation. A military operation of feeding and preparation began when he was hardly over the door. I had vaguely hoped he would leave it a day, but, as he explained, he was off back home the morrow for his family trip abroad. It was now or never. We would have to go with him. It would be miserable. And I had done the bloody mountain anyway.

Davie and I tried to kick-start some flow of adrenalin in our sluggard selves. Using the Dominie.

Carnmore, with A' Mhaighdean behind

'Do ye no like yer pals, or something?' queried Davie, 'Compleating in a place like this, hunners o miles fae the road, in weather like this? And no beer.'

'And,' I hinted darkly, 'there's a hidden agenda here. There's nae real need for this. It's a camouflage tae save the reputation of a man o dubious honour...

'No, no,' riposted the Dominie, 'It says in the book I compleated this year—and there are still four months to go.'

'How can ye say ye've compleated something in the future?' I asked, then added, 'So we don't need to go then? We can dae a wee Corbett instead withoot yer honour being held in question?'

He flinched, stiffened, gazed into the imaginary distance in the way I fancy Empire-builders did a century ago, and said, 'I am going. You don't need to come if you don't want to'—though he knew we would. We were not going to miss the chance to moan at him all the way to the top, snap at his Achilles heel. This might be the only chance we would ever get. I could not see him being so reckless, so rash again—'Temporarily Like Achilles', as the Dylan song has it.

We set off for our mountain by a fine man-made path, which crosses towards Shenaval, accompanied by the ubiquitous German doing the walk from Poolewe to Dundonnel. We warned him about rivers as we left him. Carnmore Crag behind us was like the dripping, ferocious jaws of a mythical beast as we rose up into the corrie between A' Mhaighdean and Ruadh Stac Mor. The Monklanders decided to do a circuit of both hills, but Davie and I grumpily said we'd see them at the col. It was freezing there in the driven mist, but luckily we found a wee *gîte* to shelter in and eat our supplies.

'Yon Carnmore Crag is something,' I said. 'And there's supposed tae be a big, lang V. Diff. that even we could dae on it.'

'Aye,' came back Davie, 'But when will we ever be back here?'

The Mafia arrived and we hastened on in the cold and damp to the summit of the Dominie's last Munro. There was no reason to hang about in the perishing cold, so we had a quick libation to celebrate, took a few photos, and began the descent to the bothy.

'Ye'd a narrow escape there,' I said to the world's newest compleat man, 'If ye'd broken a leg or something, ye would have been no honest man come Monday.'

But I suppose, for the honour of the Club, we would probably have carried him up in that event.

Back at Carnmore, we feasted before getting down to our celebrations. While we were eating, we chatted to a party of University students who had been at the bothy for several days, and seemed incapable of getting off their double Karrimats and Li-Los to get outside. The reason they pleaded—and they had the ironmongery to prove it—was that they were 'climbing', and of course the weather was unsuitable. This seemed to justify them doing bugger all else. When we explained our motives for being there, there was a general—as you sometimes get from young men, especially when they are in the company of their females—deprecatory attitude to the mountain habits of what they doubtless saw as old men.

Normally Davie is good at sorting out such young pups, with a few dropped references to the Piz Badile or Yosemite, but he had done nothing at Carnmore. I decided to engineer a situation for the sake of our collective honour.

'What had you intended doing?' I asked the youngsters.

Despite their recumbent habits of the past few days, they rattled off some of the most awe-inspiring names of climbs on that most awe-inspiring of crags. Now Erchie is non-competitive, and always willing to offer advice, which he did here, with good will.

'Aye, Carnmore Corner is great. But see when ye are doing Dragon, make sure ye...'

While he gave them useful advice, should they ever leave their Karrimats, they stared in amazement at the figure giving it. And learned, I think (I hope) a lesson. And they shared in our drink later on, observing the celebrations.

We had no beer, but plenty of whisky which helped to keep us warm in the spartan doss, and a wee sing-song too. But I had thought the occasion merited something special, and had composed an epic poem in the Dominie's honour, engraved on a scroll and presented to him after its reading. That night its recipient slept the Sleep of the Just. Just.

Possibly as punishment for all the arrows I had launched at the Dominie's Achilles heel, my own Achilles tendons were now giving me so much pain I could not walk wearing my boots. I donned trainers for the walk back out, and even with lighter packs it took us just under four hours next day. The weather had lifted a little, but only by turning and looking back were we able to relive the epic scene. It was something, not fearing the fate of Lot's wife, we did often.

We did go to Skye, but didn't see it for mist. Except for late one evening when Window Buttress became temporarily visible from the Glen Brittle camp site, raising our hopes that we might get a climb the next day. We gave it three days and went home.

'That's jist you left tae compleat noo, Davie,' I pointed out.

'I've been calculating,' he said. 'At my present rate o ticking aff, I might just finish aboot my hundredth birthday.'

'That soon?' I remarked, but he didn't seem to hear me.

Echo:
Greeks Bearing Gifts

The Trojans learned to 'beware Greeks bearing gifts' and it seems to me that a similar caution should be exercised towards the new breed of landowner who is using the argument of being the custodian of the wilderness, partly to justify privilege and partly to control the activities of those who visit wild areas. In the long walk into and out of Carnmore, I had the opportunity to think a little about this.

The first three miles to Kernsary, the keeper's house, showed all the familiar warnings: regular No Cars and No Fishing signs (or rather, No Fishing unless you are well-off enough to pay for it, though how anyone can own flowing water has never been explained to me).Then there were other signs, repeated when we got to Carnmore Bothy below A' Mhaighdean—less familiar signs: No Camping and No Bikes. These, as many unwary readers would be unaware, can only be in the nature of requests, unlike No Fishing signs which have legal backing. The right to camp without damage or to use rights of way with non-powered vehicles exists in Scotland. Or did. It is as yet unclear whether landowners will be able to use the new crime—invented by a Conservative government's Criminal Justice Bill—of 'aggravated trespass' against cyclists and campers.

I was reminded by these signs that the estate's owner, Paul van Vlissingen, had recently caused controversy by erecting signs which, in addition to forbidding bikes and camping, had also added 'Walkers Keep to the Footpaths' (he has obviously never walked into Carnmore, as for much of the way no path exists and such an instruction would be impossible to follow!) Afterwards these unenforceable instructions were withdrawn, but Mr Vlissingen did, in letters to such journals as *High*, attempt to defend his policies by arguing that they were necessary to conserve the wilderness and its wildlife. Unfortunately he then rather undermined his own case by proposing to bulldoze a road to near the Fionn Loch in the 'wilderness' in order to support sheep-farming—which is one of the least environmentally-friendly economic activities in an area like this! And it is impossible to argue that campers disturb wildlife, e.g. nesting birds, while fishermen and deer-stalkers do not. The difference is, surely, that the latter bring in money to the owner of the estate, while the former do not.

Mr Vlissingen has reduced over-grazing by deer on the estate,by culling more effectively than most landowners, and has spent £12,000 on restoring the bothy at Carnmore for general use, measures to be applauded. But the whole issue highlights the danger we now face of landowners—'good' or bad—jumping on the environmental bandwagon as a means of restricting access, when the old 'bugger off' methods no longer work. We should not have to depend on the goodwill of landowners for access, nor hope that Highland estates will get good, benevolent plutocrats as owners, as opposed to bad ones. Many latch too easily onto the racial argument: it is foreigners, whether Dutch multi-millionaries in Letterewe, or Gulf sheikhs in Kintail, who are the problem. Little do they know their history: the bulk of the nineteenth century clearing landlords were Scottish.

The outcome to the whole controversy over Letterewe was an agreement between Mr Vlissingen and various conservationist and recreational bodies, dubbed the 'Letterewe Accord.' It would be churlish not to welcome its recommendations. The estate pledges itself against the use of tracked vehicles in favour of e.g. ponies, and downgrades the hunting aspect of the estate in favour of a conservation programme. On the other hand walkers are encouraged to use 'the long walk in', to avoid damaging fires and camping in sensitive areas—most of which is standard practice for most mountaineers anyway. The right of access is enshrined, subject to essential estate work.

But let us put this in perspective. The likelihood of more than a handful of private landlords following this example is non-existent. Most will continue to use land as a speculative investment and/or an environmentally damaging sporting asset, and will be tempted to use their increased powers under law to restrict access. But even in the case of Letterewe, we are still hostage to the owner's wishes, which may eventually be whims. Landowners can get fed up of playing at environmental restoration, and move on to another hobby. Or they can have financial difficulties and change priorities, or even sell to someone not sharing their philosophy.

Around the halfway stage of the walk in, talk turned to the history of the estate, and its most famous landlord who had himself bothied at Carnmore, Osgood Mackenzie. Now there was a candidate for the 'Good Scottish laird' if ever there was one! Enthusiast for the Gaelic, chronicler of Highland customs and turner of the barren promontory of Inverewe into a Mecca for botanists and gardeners worldwide. But read his *A Hundred Years in the Highlands* and the surprise is that there is anything alive in the whole area: if it moved, he killed it! To plough through the frenzied orgy of blood-letting described in this book is a stomach-churning experience:

>...my total in that year [1868] was 1,314 grouse, 33 black game, 49 partridges, 110 golden plover, 35 ducks, 53 snipe, 91 blue-rock pigeons, 184 hares without mentioning geese, teal, ptarmigan and roe etc., a total of 1,900 head...Now many of these good beasts are extinct or on the verge of becoming so. (p. 185)

No wonder, with slaughter on that scale! Slaughter paralleled by massive over-fishing with the same depletive results.

And we are not just talking of game, of which he describes the countless amounts massacred. We are also talking about what he classed as 'vermin' and systematically eradicated with his keepers: foxes, badgers, pine marten, sea eagles and ospreys—whose eggs he took—wild cat and polecat, all reduced or wiped out with trap and dog and strychnine—'a wonderfully handy drug' he calls it. Pity it hadn't got into his hip-flask. Convinced that it was not his own wholesale slaughter which was reducing the numbers of fish and fowl, but the actions of their natural predators, to his father's boast of having exterminated the fork-tailed kite he proudly adds his own: that 'The pine martens, polecats and the badgers are all quite extinct with us now...'(p. 64); and fulminates against attempts to protect the eagle from persecution. So far from being the pioneer of conservation portrayed in the sanitised exhibition at Inverewe Gardens, he should be seen as an agent of ecological disaster. It would have been a greater legacy to us, had Osgood Mackenzie spent his time and money restoring the natural flora of the estate and planting native species, rather than playing silly games at Inverewe while destroying the native wildlife. But that is wishful thinking, a retrospective pious hope.

We should not have to rely on hope that the owners of land will be its best custodians: but private ownership of the land leaves us hostage to this hope. There is a multitude of alternatives: co-operative crofters' ownership, ownership by charitable organisations like the John Muir

Trust, by the National Trust or by the state through agencies like Scottish Natural Heritage, all of which might one day, as Marx said, 'make the ownership of land by an individual seem as absurd as the ownership of one human being by another'—or even as the ownership of running water and the fruits thereof! But in the meantime, 'beware landlords posing as benefactors' and be prepared to assert rights of access, tempered by informed environmental concern.

July
MOTHER'S DAY

The trouble with having a companion in life who, like Caesar's wife, is beyond reproach, is that one feels all the more acutely one's inability to be Caesar.

Erchie would whiles say, in giving expression to his view that the aim of the female is to veto male activity (a fate which only the constant vigilance of bachelorhood has avoided for him), 'Ye are very lucky, ye know. Most wives wouldnae let their men away as often as you get.'

Davie however would bring mature clarification to the issue, and after pointing out that my companion 'radiated serenity', explained,

'No, no, it's no that. She's daen a lot hersel, nearly as mony Munros as I have. And a bit o climbin. Aonach Eagach in the winter, Central Gully on Ben Lui...'

And the Dominie would chip in, pointing out how fortunate I was to have someone so knowledgeable in irregular Gaelic verbs. He would often phone her up when I was out to discuss Gaelic declension and gerunds with her, solving his little problems.

All this rather defeats one of the main objects of going away with the Big Boys: having a guid greet aboot the missus. I kept my secret sorrows to myself. It would have been disloyal to say that 'she' only wanted to see the back of me now, and that the early activities were in order to 'get her man'—then abandoned once she had. But heading for Pinnacle Ridge on Sgurr nan Gillean, I knew it was more complicated. Not indeed that she intended to climb the Ridge with Kevin and myself, she was just coming out for a walk from the hotel to its base. She had her own agenda for coming.

And she still came. True, not in winter any more; true, never to bothies. Days out in summer, or longer trips to hotels with forays to new summits. And (I knew) because she wanted to. Not that she had any desire to 'stand by her man'. Damn it, she had just been on a course at the Gaelic College in Skye, while I had had a couple of sun-soaked weeks on the Pyrenees. We met up at the hotel, and had, for me, a wonderful day driving round Skye watching the torrential rain and mist—how I longed for that in the Pyrenees. But the next morning was splendid. I had arranged to meet an old pal, Kevin, now resident in Skye, for a scramble over Pinnacle Ridge. We met at Sligachan Hotel, and set off over the moor. The summits were clear, and there was a great bustle of people preparing for the hills: but we didn't see any of them on our trip.

After swopping the usual what-you-been-doing chat with Kevin, I pointed out to my life-partner that one of the early ascents of Sgurr nan Gillean had been by her namesake, John Mackenzie, when he was ten years old. Later he made the first ascent of Sgurr a Ghreadaidh. Mackenzie had operated as a guide from the hotel we had just left for fifty years, never having an accident with a client. As well as guiding, the Sconser crofter did much exploratory work in the Cuillin, mainly with Norman Collie. In 1896 they climbed Sgurr Coire an Lochain, the last unclimbed peak in Britain. They discovered the Cioch in Coire Lagain together, and joined many of the 'gaps' in the Ridge, like the Thearlaich-Dubh gap. Sgurr Mhic Choinnich, one of the finest Cuillin peaks, is named after him. She should model herself on him, I suggested.

'He was probably a relative,' was her comment, and this was, in her clan consciousness, probably to her the most important thing about him.

Kevin, who did a bit of guiding himself, had taken us quickly to the bottom of the first of the five pinnacles of our ridge, after wending our way up Coire a Bhasteir. On our left a massive gorge carried the furious Allt Dearg Beag in a dark chasm. We had walked into thin mist a little lower down, but now it had thickened. We waited a while, and soon it was clear that it would not clear. Kevin asked her, 'Can you find the way down?'

'Oh, I'll just come with you,' she said, imperturbable as ever, and trusting: 'It's quite easy, isn't it?'

While I looked at her, realising again how simple it must have been for the chiefs to steal all the Highlanders' lands, Kevin had replied, assuring her that it was mostly just a scramble. We set off over the easy-angled black gabbro of the First Pinnacle in the enveloping mist. That proceeded without hitch, as did the ascent of the Second Pinnacle. Though there was nothing to see but mist and gabbro, we were all enjoying the scramble, and the Jurassic feel of the Cuillin. I said, 'It'll be no problem if the weather doesn't get any worse.'

But it did. The trouble started as we were ascending the Third Pinnacle, when the mist intensified to light rain, and visibility shrank even further. By the time we reached the top, and the abseil point for the descent of the trickiest part of the climb, the heavens had opened and it was pouring as hard as any of the brief Pyrenean thunderstorms I had recently witnessed. I hoped, without any rational basis, that this downpour would be as brief.

Ahead, sharper towers loomed through the mist, which they wrapped around them like a tattered garment. Their ill-concealed black nakedness was intimidating, not enticing.

We had a choice. We could go on and hope it improved, or we could retreat. The latter would take just as long now as getting to the summit, and retreat would give us a route-finding problem in the mist. Whereas from the summit, the Tourist Path would lead us securely back to the hotel. She said, calmly, as Kevin and I discussed it:

'I like the sound of that. A Tourist Path. Let's go on.'

We had the rope, but I did not fancy the abseil over rocks running with water. Though I'm not the world's best abseiler, I've done it; my life-partner had not, and this was not the place to learn. Kevin's skill and knowledge of the route enabled us to descend over steep, but sound rock, and then to re-ascend by a gully, only semi-rotten by Cuillin standards, to the base of Knight's Peak, our Fourth Pinnacle.

The swirling mist was raw, and we were all frozen, fingers numbed from the cold rock. And we were all wet, wetter than I have ever been. The rain bucketed down, and the entire Cuillin was a huge water-slide. It ran into your boots, it ran down your sleeves. There wasn't a dry centimetre on any of us. But it was epic, mist and rain twisting round the dark gabbro monoliths. And we were lucky it was gabbro, for on no other rock would we have maintained such adhesion in such conditions.

'Watch the wee light bits,' I warned her, 'They are slippy'—feeling I could leave the geology lesson about the basalt intrusions till later.

Neither Knight's Peak nor the final Pinnacle are very difficult, but they are steep in places, with severe exposure—much of which we were luckily spared by the mist. She climbed. Looking always upwards, not sideways or down. Always having three points of contact with the rock. At the trickiest point on Knight's Peak she hesitated, trembled a little and said—to herself I think, 'This is no place for a mammy to be.'

Eventually we were shivering on the summit. I congratulated her. She now had a couple of Cuillin peaks under her belt and should set her eyes on that named after her fellow Mackenzie next. She gave me that 'never again' look I have seen from her on many hills. But she would dine on it for months, be able to say of Pinnacle Ridge what John Mackenzie had said of the Inaccessible Pinnacle:

'I know it's impossible: I've been up it ma'sel!'

Pinnacle Ridge, Sgurr nan Gillean

Now came the Tourist Path, a bugger on the best of days. A knee-wrenching, soul-destroying grind over loose boulders and scree. As we descended into Coire Riabhach the mist relented a little, we could see over the moor towards the hotel. But the rain continued, still it fell in unforgiving mercilessness. She wanted to stop, but it could have been dangerous with the cold, it was necessary to keep going. Of my companion, you could say, as Collie said of Mackenzie, with a sexual correction, '[s]he was...a most loveable, charming and delightful companion...who never offended by word or deed.'

But the day's hardship eventually produced a minor registering of protest. When refused a rest, she said, 'If I'd have known, I wouldn't have come.'

Did she mean, I asked, known about the ordeals of Pinnacle Ridge?

'No, about this Tourist Path!'

We ground on and on, ever downwards, over the footbridge we needed because of the boiling, cascading river, towards the hotel, which we eventually reached. There we stripped off our clothes, poured the water out of our boots. Then I saw, as the flaps of her shirt-tail failed to cover it, my wife's bare arse. Now she shares a little of the prudishness of her race, and I was astonished, until I saw her wringing splashes of water out of her knickers. It was that wet.

In the Pyrenees I had done theoretically bigger days, and repeated them without a rest-day. It took four full days to recover from the aquaeous ascent of Pinnacle Ridge—a single good Scottish day out. We toddled about Skye a couple of more days, and made a run to Glen Brittle, to show the conquistadorette of Pinnacle Ridge Coire Lagain and Mackenzie's Peak. Though we were still too stiff and tired to stir far from the car, we did take a walk over the suspension bridge to the old croft houses of Glenbrittle, to look upwards. From the long stare she gave, I felt she might possibly be on the Cuillin again.

Echo:
Glenbrittle: Climbers and Crofters

This time I had started my Cuillin scramble from the Sligachan Hotel, where many of the pioneers of Skye mountaineering had resided. In the Victorian era Sligachan was the centre of Cuillin exploration, and Mackenzie had guided his clients from the hotel doors. But Sligachan was soon to lose its pre-eminence, and the nature of climbing was to change with the democratic explosion between the wars.

Mackenzie had guided the rich upper classes of the Victorian and Edwardian eras. They thought very highly of him—as a typical entry in the Sligachan Visitors' Book shows, describing him as 'a capital climber' who 'may without hesitation be strongly recommended as a guide.' Yet Mackenzie was employed—and clearly in the role of a servant. In photographs he is always deferentially a little behind, or to the side of, his clients, and he had the task of carrying the supplies and equipment on the hill. Back at the hotel, he had to eat with the domestics 'below' while the gentlemen ate in the lounge—and he had to get himself to Sconser and back to the hotel in the morning, under his own foot power, after a day on the hill. A six mile round trip.

Mackenzie's deep relationship with Collie, beside whom he is buried at Struan, has often been commented on. But even Collie found it impossible to invite his friend into the dining room or bar of the Sligachan Hotel, to mingle with the lawyers, industrialists and others who made up the élite mountaineering world of class-bound late Victorian and Edwardian society. Things were more demotic when the focus in Skye moved to the southern Cuillin, and Coire Lagain.

A hundred years ago Glen Brittle was one of the least visited parts of Skye. But with the increase in mountain exploration in the Cuillin, which led to the appearance of A. P. Abraham's *Rock Climbing in Skye* in 1908, all this changed. Glen Brittle soon replaced Sligachan as the main centre for Cuillin climbers, who came in increasing numbers. The problem was, there was limited accommodation in Glen Brittle, which lacked a hotel. But a little local ingenuity helped out, and a harmonious relationship emerged between climbers and crofters.

The first to offer accommodation was the shepherd at Glen Brittle Cottage, Ewan Campbell—or rather his sister Mary, who started providing food and shelter for mountaineers in 1906, and continued till her death in 1947. In the early days climbers slept in a bed recess in the living room, where a sign warned them of 'The Unseen Guest At Every Meal. The Silent Listener To Every Conversation'. Later a sleeping annexe was built and a lounge provided for the climbers.

Mary's hospitality was legend, as was her cooking, to which her visitors' book bore ample testimony, as for example:

Mary, fair maid of Glen Brittle
We thank you not a little
For comfort and care
The smile ever there
And plenty of excellent victual.

J.H.B. Bell recorded that after he had been fed, 'Mary entered with a second meal of two boiled eggs, scones and tea,' which he also polished off. Amongst her most frequent visitors were the climbers and authors of the Scottish Mountaineering Club *Guide to Skye*, Steeple and Barlow. They were so impressed that they inserted into the guide to climbs on the Cuillin the comment that 'numerous climbers recall with delight the hospitality received at the hands of Mary Campbell.' But the *Guide* also mentions that 'it is possible to obtain good accommodation at the Post Office in Glen Brittle'. Competition had arrived—and Mary put up a sign advertising CAMPBELL'S SEASIDE HOSTEL at the entrance to the Glen.

From 1912 another hostel was provided by Mrs Chisholm, whose family had the Post Office on the west side of the river. This proved equally popular with the ever-increasing number of vistors, over three-quarters of whom even then came from south of the border. In the days when supplies were more difficult to get than now, one of Mrs Chisholm's tasks was to be the custodian of the masses of provisions which climbers sent in advance to her little post office. Amongst her guests were Ben Humble, author of *The Cuillin of Skye*, and A. E. Robertson. But her most famous was probably George Mallory in 1918, later to perish on Everest.

The further increase in outdoor activity in the 1930s meant yet more bed-space was needed. Glen Brittle House had occasionally been hired 'for the season' by well-off gentlemen such as Norman Collie before 1914. In 1931 Mr MacRae, manager of Glen Brittle farm, took the tenancy of the House and opened it for climbers. This was obviously a more comfortable establishment than the cottages of the Campbells or the Chisholms, and Tom Weir mentions coming off the hill to 'a bath and dinner'—when a climber at the Campbells' wanted a wash, he had to go to the burn for it! The MacRaes later set up the first bus service from Glen Brittle, and the swell of climbers was such that the Carbost grocer started a twice a week delivery to the Glen in summer.

Various other expedients eased the problem of accommodation. The school, on the same side of the river as the Chisholms', was used as a Hostel in the summer holidays, and there was a 'tiny shed with four beds and a stove' run by the Sutherland family as well, according to Ben Humble. But with the passing away of the older generation after 1945, things inevitably, but sadly, became more organised. The Youth Hostels Association opened a 90-bed building, to be followed by a smaller one built by the British Mountaineering Council. There is now also bunk-house style accommodation provided by a long-term resident climbing instructor in the Glen. But the days of the Chisholms, Campbells and MacRaes are gone. We can read about them, but alas that is all.

And, though present arrangements might lack the romance of living with Gaelic-speaking natives, it is certain that no-one who visits Glen Brittle for the Cuillin would wish to see the glen desecrated by a Visitor Centre, Heritage Centre or whatever it is called, as has been proposed by the Macleod Estates. For whatever it is called, such a development will be simply a staging post on the bus-tour knick-knack circuit. Let's leave local people and climbers to solve any accommodation problems that arise, as they have traditionally done, without the intrusion of landlord-inspired commercial initiatives.

August:
FATHER'S DAYS

When I saw the ghetto blaster and the Rangers' strips, I sensed this was going to be no ordinary trip: later sighting of a Partick Thistle strip reassured me only a little.

Hoist on a petard of my own making from which I could hardly, with honour, escape, I was taking a group of—if not the threatened Five Boys—at least four, on a bothy trip. Only one of the boys was mine.

Mine was the source of the problem: the others averaged five years older than him and he was bottom of the pecking order. To correct this, he had doubtless been boasting about his mountain days and bothy nights. This had led to vague demands from his pals—which I felt it safe enough to accede to—to come along sometime. Eventually I was cornered, and agreed to a trip. I had expected some moral and physical support from the other members of the Stobcross Gentlemen's Mountaineering Club, but they were strangely evasive this time—and on subsequent meets with the 'Bash Street Kids' as one wit had christened my recently acquired charges.

'Na, its mair like Lord Snooty and his Pals,' I commented, swopping dimly-remembered comparisons from D.C.Thomson *Dandy* and *Beano* days of my own youth. For my son's pals were miles behind the superbly-equipped, over-privileged and mountain-cognisant kid of ten who had leapfrogged the status ladder of the mean streets. These were inner-city kids, lovely kids and street-wise, but already knowing some of the issues of the dole, of one-parenthood, of problems with schooling.

But nothing of the big wide world of the mountains.

I looked at the footwear: one pair of mountain boots, one of trainers and a pair of bovver-type boots. But we could get away with that on the hill I had planned. One rucksack, but plenty of plastic bags, and a hold-all. But we could get off with that as we were driving to the bothy. 'Keep it simple', I kept telling myself. Outside the rucksack hung pans, cups and other paraphernalia—and a hammer and a screwdriver.

'Whit's that for?' I queried, trying to understand the mind of the young, increasingly a mystery to me, 'Vampires?'

'I though we might need that, oot there in the wilds,' came the reply.

I decided to do a quick grub check. Of course it was Mars Bars, Irn-Bru, crisps and tins of beans, but for a couple of days they would survive. To the bovver-booted hold-all carrier I addressed my question concerning his provisions.

'Ravioli,' he said.

'Aye, that's for yer tea, but whit aboot breakfast?'

'Ravioli,' he answered, looking puzzled.

'And for the hill?' I asked, knowing the answer would be—'Ravioli.'

A Dreary Drumochter would do them, I thought, as we headed up the A9, with what sounded like a techno rave going on in the back seat. I found myself saying it before I could bite my tongue:

'When we were your age, we had good music, wi proper tunes and wurds. The Beatles, Bob Dylan...'

They did not appear to hear, but I consoled myself that the weather appeared to be holding fine, though cool. As we stopped at a lay-by, I was hoping my leadership skills were enough to get this motley crew up Sgairneach Mhor. Then I heard the banging: the gentry were out at the grouse. My heart sank—I could see me taking the kids home to their mammies, full of buckshot.

After describing the route to them, I gave them strict instructions to stay with me for the duration. My own and another who peched and puffed his way to the top in two hours did. But I had forgotten the sheer animal physicality of adolescent boys. Chaining them would be the only way to restrain them, and the other two raced off towards the summit at a speed I could never now match, in order to be down in time for the football commentary on the car radio.

Luckily the shooters and their dogs were on A' Mharconaich, and though we saw and heard them all day, we did not cross their path. It is a toil through heather to the top of Sgairneach Mhor, but the Bash Street Kids seemed to enjoy it. The one peching and puffing beside me said it was the most beautiful view he had ever seen in his life, though he revised it when he got to the top, and the landscape opened out. At one point he said to me, 'In Gothic times, they would have done this in bare feet'—showing he had a sense of history, as well as of beauty.

The others had waited for us at the top, where they eagerly questioned me about what they could see, the names of all the other hills beyond Loch Ericht and Ben Alder. Then one said,

'I suppose if it was really clear, we would see the Pacific Ocean?'

I didn't feel in pedantic enough mode to contradict him over this, but did insist that the bullets he had heard had NOT been whistling about his ears, and not even to think about mentioning bullets of any description to his mammy, or he would be in greater danger from me than from any bullet. At this point the Big Yin asked,

'Gie's yer car keys and we'll go doon and listen to the fitba.'

Now, unchuffed as I was at this easy assumption of familiarity, I reflected that unless youth ask for and take equality they will never get it, so with the usual 'mixing a' with admonition due' I handed the keys over and watched their flight off the hill, wishing I could still move like that.

Back at the car we sunned ourselves and listened to the football results, before going to the Dalwhinnie Transport Cafe for, as I thought, some sustenance. But as I and my biological charge sat sensibly eating together, the others squandered their spending money on the pool table, which I only managed to drag them away from when their funds were exhausted. I felt that, somehow, control of this whole learning experience was slipping away from me...

Even more so when we got to Melgarve, and I had thought of establishing fatigue parties for wood, water and cooking. No chance, I was left to do all that as they disappeared, in a resurgence of puppy animality, for a swim in the Spey, only slightly to be chastened when they found they were sharing their pool with a dead sheep. When I saw the spray-on deodorants after the swim I thought I had seen everything—though most of their sweet smells were lost in the acrid reek caused by their later attempts to fry sausage slice without any fat.

Evening was passed in fire-watching, magic to kids brought up in the Smokeless Era, and in story telling. Now I don't regard myself as a great story teller, but managed in response to demand to scrape up and re-hash a few Poe and Maupassant tales, dimly-remembered, and they went down a bomb. So much so that a couple of the Kids, who had intended to sleep in another room, borrowed the torch to go and collect their sleeping bags and bring them into the collective security of the one with the fire...

Next morning they all disappeared for an exploration of the source of the Spey for three hours, while I tidied the doss and packed up. Much to my surprise they all returned alive, demanding to stay another day. I pointed out we had no food.

'We can catch fish,' suggested one, without irony—and suddenly I was back thirty years, with Desperate Dan, full of daft ideas and doing daft things at the same age. But now I know the fish always gets away, so we went home.

That is it, I thought. I've done it. If Purgatory exists, I must have earned maximum remission. In fact, maybe that *was* Purgatory? But the day after returning, my wife, with a very superior and knowing smile told me, 'Your pals are at the door.'

A delegation. In back-to-front baseball caps, football strips and trainers.

'When we goin again? Can we go next week? For a full week-end this time?'

'Gissa break! Away ye go and beat up old ladies and sniff glue! We'll see,' I replied, forcing the row of trainers off the doorstep, and closing the door.

Being popular is nice, but it has its problems. I thought over the winter they might forget their trip, but spring brought a renewed demand for a weekend away.

I tried to buy them off with a few days out, but this merely whetted their appetites, so eventually I decided—to avoid the strain of driving a mobile disco—to take them in over the Rannoch Moor to Staonaig by train. I had a Family Railcard, and could get them all there and back for a quid each on it.

'You must be mad,' said my wife, giving a female angle on the issue. 'Can't you just drink and chase women, like other men of your age?'

Trying to explain to women that there are other things in life than seeking one's own comfort and self-interest, such as duty and honour, is something I gave up on long ago.

If the last trip was Purgatory, this one promised to be Paradise. The weather was perfect on the journey to Corrour station, where most who decanted from the train headed hostel-wards. And dropping to Loch Trieg we were blessed with as fine a summer's evening as one could wish. At Craigeunach Lodge I rested amongst the trees, while the lads bounce-bombed with stones off the rickety bridge. I vaguely felt I should be telling them to desist from behaviour which did not seem to fit into the Spiritual Odyssey view of mountain life, but couldn't be bothered. They were enjoying themselves.

The bothy was empty when we arrived, but their animal energies were not exhausted, and they went, like a pack of seals, for a swim in the pool in the river. In the evening one of them asked, 'Whyssis bothy pure far away fae the station?'

And I explained that it had not been built as a bothy, but like the other houses on the route through to Fort William (Craigeunach, Luibeilt, Meanach and Steall) the building had housed a shepherd or a gamekeeper—or a stationmaster, as at Corrour itself. Six habitations fifty years ago in an area where only Old Morgan at Corrour remains.

And no-one will follow the redundant stationmaster when he goes from the unmanned station. He was a character, the wild-eyed, grey shock-haired man, who had refused to pay his poll-tax since he had no road, no lighting, no refuse-collection and no children at school. A character too was the Hostel Warden, Old Tom, who had looked after Corrour Youth Hostel for decades and knew the area and its lore intimately. He still ran round Loch Ossian, eight miles, in less than an hour every day, and had a pet stag he fed by hand. The hills were still producing their mythical figures, I pointed out.

I had kept their attention, but you don't want to overdo it, so they went off for a scramble over the rocks above Staonaig before bed-time. Which gave me a chance at a furtive few drams.

We trekked to Meanach the next day, where we had a wee stop. Across the river was Luibuilt, falling further into ruin. I don't think they believed me when I told them I had seen it inhabited, twenty years before. The day was splendid, clear blue skies but with a cooling breeze to ease walking, and we made good time up the firm stalker's path from Meanach towards Stob Ban, our chosen peak.

Though it was a fine summer, it had followed a hard winter, and as we rose we gained views towards Binnein Mhor, where the snow still sloped below the summit ridge. I recalled the time years ago when, in July, in gymshoes (I was suffering from Achilles Tendon) I had run from Staonaig to Binnein Mhor, exulting in my fitness, only to be defeated below the summit by steep hard snow on which my gymshoes would not grip. Further over the lads gasped in appreciation as the ridges and snowfields of the Aonachs and Ben Nevis appeared level with our gaze. I myself had never seen so much snow in Scotland in July. We even found our own mini-snowfield on the way to the summit of Stob Ban, which is a full 1,000 ft. lower than Ben Nevis.

We took the route back by the Lairig Leacach and Craigeunach, partly because it is a lovely gorge and wood walk I wanted the kids to see. And partly because that way lay firewood, and I was determined that this time they would hew wood and draw water for their sins. It was a clear sky, it would be a cold night. A bleeze would do just nicely. As it happened, they were so enthusiastic in their labours that we left enough wood for several subsequent parties.

I was knackered: that had been quite a long round trip, maybe fourteen miles all told. Happily, after eating they left me to sip from my hip-flask of comfort, and went off for further ritual ablutions in the Abhainn Ra. This time I joined them, found that their claims that the water was warm were true, and had my most enjoyable outdoor swim in many years.

Gratifying as one's duties to the future of Scottish mountaineering can be, it is nice to pretend to be a grown-up every now and again. Therefore I was delighted when that evening I had adult company in the form of a lad who had just come over the Aonachs from the Fort, and dropped into the bothy. We could establish adult space, talk about adult things, find out we had mutual acquaintances, swop beer for whisky, chat about climbing.

Maybe it was recognising that in that department the newcomer was clearly out of my league that spurred the Kids to intervene, to defend their leader. Pointing to me, one said,

'He's wrote books, ye know.'

Once the mock-modesty of my explanation was over, I discovered I had a reader in my fellow adult, and further pleasant chat ensued.

The weather broke next day, and caught us in a chilling downpour on the slog back to Corrour, where we waited for the train, cold and wet, with those who had week-ended in the hostel as companions.

On the train I thought I deserved a break, so I deposited the Bash Street contingent together at a table, and distanced myself from them, heading for the Buffet Trolley, where I treated myself to goodies full of chocolate and fat, and to a few wee miniatures of the craitur. Food and drink gradually drove away the feeling of cold in a rising warmth. But my reverie was shattered by the cry of the ticket-inspector in my eardrums. He clearly felt he had discovered a fraud, for he looked at me with a steely eye and asked,

'Issat lot back there wi nae tickets wi you? They say they are wi you?'

I looked down the train at my charges, then at the ticket-inspector, with a benign glow of collective responsibility surging through me and, pulling out my Railcard with all the properly paid-for and validated tickets, answered,

'Aye, ye could say they were wi me. They are All my Sons.'

I do try. And bore the arse off them saying how independent I was at their age, cycling to Skye and back. Encourage them to paddle their own proverbial canoes. But they seem to have no desire to go it alone, seem to like leadership. I suggested to Davie, who is very intrigued by the Bash Street Kids (in the breach, not the observance), that it must be another of the terrible effects of Thatcherism, this lack of independence in the youth. He looked at me sagely and replied (I must say, without any apparent sympathy),

'Na, its no that. Ye've jist made a rod for yer ain back, that's whit. A rod fer yer ain back.'

Echo:
Memories of Penmeanach and Ardnish

On another occasion, I fulfilled paternal obligations with a friend and our collection of children, visiting Ardnish for a first time to stay at Penmeanach bothy. From Loch Beag the path rose steeply to over 600 ft. before descending from the moor. Our track gave signs at several points of having been formerly maintained, with a series of semi-paved step-like parts. I found myself wondering who could have carried out all this labour in such a remote part of the West Highlands.

Almost all mountain bothies I had previously visited were isolated ex-shepherd's/gamekeeper's/forester's cottages, but it was immediately clear that the Penmeanach bothy was the survivor of an actual village. I counted at least seven separate buildings arranged in a crescent, with the unmistakeable signs of regular lazybed cultivation down to the shore, and drained rough grazing behind the settlement. Wanderings over the peninsula during the next two days revealed many other signs of economic activity: amongst them a sheep-fank and a rude harbour with pier. Clearly, the Ardnish peninsula had at one time maintained a large local population, though now only one holiday home remains for its present owner, at Laggan.

On returning home, I looked up the Crofters' (Napier) Commission Report of 1885, and luckily there was an entry for Penmeanach (Beinmeanach)—penny-land (or hill) of the middle-field. Interestingly, the evidence on Penmeanach was collected by Sheriff Nicolson, the Skyeman who was the first to climb both Sgurr Alasdair and Sgurr Dubh in the Cuillin. The Report confirmed that there were seven families in Penmeanach, as well as another twelve in the settlements of Glasnacardaich, Laggan, Marlachbui, Slock and Feorlain-due, all of which can still be located on the O.S. map. This would possibly indicate a population on the peninsula at that time of around 100-150, based on an average family size of 5-7.

Rents averaged between £5 and £10 per croft, with £22 for a 'farmer' at Feorlain-due. Holdings were small and could not pay the rent: the main source of income for the crofters was gathering shellfish, which earned them about 5s (25p) a week. Also the penetration of the High-lands by the railways had cut their income from droving to the lowlands. As well as complaints about the onerous level of the rents, the tenants were aggrieved at the large areas set aside for deer forest, and the crowd-ing of the crofters onto smaller and worthless scraps of land, with the attendant evictions of families. A petition was presented to the Croft-ers' Commission by Allan MacDonald, Ronald McEachen 'and fifteen others', which echoed the age-old cry of the Highland crofters:

> We know that the present rent is far too high, in fact double what it should be. We wish that in case of eviction, Government should interfere between tenant and landlord...We hold that the crofter has as much right to live on the land of his forefathers as the proprietor has to be superior over it.

Although the crofters complained of evictions from Ardnish, and of people being pressurised to leave by being refused permission to build houses (this happened to one James MacDonald), it is clear that Penmeanach settlement, and the other crofts in this inaccessible penin-sula, were themselves created by Clearances. Donald MacVarish explained this when he gave evidence to Nicolson and the other Commissioners:

> It is a matter of recent history that Penmeanach and Laggan were crofted by one man, and the present overcrowding is not from rapid multiplica-tion [but] the result of the clearing of the townships of Goadal and Ardnafuaran whose people were put in among us.

Since their own land was more valuable for sheep and deer, they were 'dumped' on the less valuable and difficult-of-access Ardnish.

A further complaint was the road—or lack of it, though the crofters had to pay a road tax—to Ardnish. As a result they had to be supplied the goods they needed by passing steamers. Donald MacVarish stated that 'It is an inaccessible place.' And indeed the lack of a road probably doomed Penmeanach and the other clachans of Ardnish, though the reduction in rents and security of tenure brought about by the Crofters Act of 1886 would undoubtedly have met many of the grievances of the population.

There was no church in the peninsula, and the famous Chapel on the Braes at Lochailort (featured in the film *Local Hero*) was built for the people of the settlements. The largely Catholic population of Ardnish would make the long walk there for worship and marriage ceremo-nies. At one time the chapel served over 300 people, including the clachans such as Polnish on the landward side of Ardnish, but it closed its doors in 1964, and awaits a purchaser and restoration.

In her charming book, *Moidart and Morar* (Moray Press, 1950), Wendy Wood wrote, 'The barren-looking promontory of Ardnish had, not so long ago, a roll of about sixty children on its school list.'

It is not clear which period she is talking about, but presumably this refers to around 1900 when population was at its maximum, for the figure soon declined. According to Mrs Nellie MacQueen (who was born in the peninsula, and who still lives in Arisaig with her son Ian) while her own mother was the teacher from just before the First World War till the closure of the school in or around 1932, the maximum roll was 28. By the latter date, when the school was closed, there were no children of school age, indicating a rapid population decline after the First World War, and an ageing population.

Mrs MacQueen's mother was originally from Barra, and came to Penmeanach to marry a local resident, who also had the Post Office. This building, missing in an 1882 photograph of the village, now houses the Mountain Bothies Association bothy. Wendy Wood must have been one of the last visitors to see it in its original form:

> The low cottage on the shore still had, when I last visited it, a wooden sign hanging by one nail, saying 'Post Office'. Just prior to the war, looking for a spot to set up a kiosk, a telephone official was setting out for Ardnish, when it was pointed out to him that there was now only one house and three people on the whole place.

With the removal of the Macdonalds in 1942 (Mrs MacQueen's family) Penmeanach became deserted: she herself initially went to Fort William to work in the aluminium factory.

Talking with Mrs MacQueen it became clear how little had changed in Penmeanach between 1885 and 1942. It was true that they then had a postal service twice a week from the postman who lived at Marlachbui, the croft nearest the main road. But they still had no phone, no electricity, and no radios—even battery operated—as she recalls. No shops, of course, and they were still served by passing steamers. They still cut their own peats, grew their own potatoes and vegetables, produced their own eggs and milk, and made their own butter as well. Fish for the families came from the sea and the hill-lochs. Apart from Mrs MacQueen's own family, who had income from the teacher's salary and the Post Office, most people's livelihood still came from collecting shellfish.

But although human life left Penmeanach, as it had done

Glasnacardoch and Marlachbui, in 1942, it hung on elsewhere in Ardnish. In the late 1960s, when Penmeanach itself was in ruins, Donald Macleod and his wife were still living at Laggan, keeping a few cows and 2,000 sheep, although the couple were both over 80. Soon afterwards, when the mailboat ceased to call at Laggan, and faced with a prohibitive charge for installing a telephone, they left the peninsula.

MacLeod had had an interesting life. Although he and his wife had been born in Harris, MacLeod, like many Highlanders, had been a gaucho tending sheep in the high cordilleras of Patagonia between the wars, before coming back to the west Highlands, where he lived at Laggan for thirty years. Of his horseback gaucho time he stated, 'These were grand days. There was freedom there.'

The building which at present houses the bothy was being used as a byre in the 1960s, and in disrepair: it was restored by the Mountain Bothies Association in 1975. It is of dressed-stone construction, superior to the rest of the village, and had a slated roof rather than a thatched one. Its existence ensures that some life, although of a different kind to that of the original inhabitants, still exists occasionally at the settlement.

Interestingly, as I left in the rain, I noticed that re-colonisation of the area had begun. Just before the railway line, a group of old ruins had been occupied by travellers, complete with horses and dogs, with smoke issuing from the tarpaulined roofs. Their conditions of life seemed little more comfortable than those of the crofters of a century ago, or than the bothy life I had just experienced for a week-end. Indeed, Mrs MacQueen's son, Ian, told me that the travellers lived by collecting shellfish, as his own forebears at Penmeanach had done. And I was glad to hear that he still kept up that link, by visiting Ardnish regularly to fish and explore a corner from which the people have gone and only their memories remain.

It was an easy week-end. A trip to the seaside for the young lads. They played in the sand, tried to swim in the freezing Atlantic, tried to find fish willing to bite from the rocks, explored the woods and collected firewood. Listened to ghost tales and songs by the fire at night. Made their own memories, and ones for us, laughing and playing where the silent dead had done before them.

September:
INDIAN SUMMER: MAD HORSES
AND SCOTSMEN

After a couple of weeks in the Stubai Alps, where I had done over 30,000 ft of ascent and descent and seen—it felt like—the same number of people, I fancied something different. Something long, but flattish—and on my own. My finger had often traced on the map an obvious route following the lines of the rivers flowing out of the Atholl mountains, linking the old drove roads through the passes of Gaick and Glen Tilt. A route which appeared trackless, and which I had never heard or read of anyone doing. It was time for my feet to follow my dreaming finger on a three-day hike through the wilds accompanied only by sex, death and madness.

I got off the train at Blair Atholl station on a mid September afternoon, and fortified myself, before starting on the first leg of the trek, at the grand tea shop in the Water Mill beside the station. The sustenance was welcome, as I was only lightly provisioned. My destination that night was the Tarf Bothy, about fifteen miles away. That far, I would be on familiar ground.

The route goes up Glen Tilt on the west side of the river from the Old Bridge of Tilt, before crossing to the east below Croftmore, recrossing again at Marble Lodge. This is a private estate road, part tarred, part Land Rover track, which makes easy walking till it reaches the stalker's house at Forest Lodge. There are a few inhabited houses in the glen, and this is the final one, eight miles from the station. In fact, Mr Pirie, the 'gamie', was the last person I saw for almost two days.

The lower reaches of the glen are delightful, with mixed woodland and deep river gorges framed by steep hillsides. Everywhere are the ruins of crofts and shielings from the days when the glen had a population of several hundred: today it has about ten. Hundreds more passed through annually, driving cattle from the Highlands to the lowland trysts (markets). Today Braemar-Blair Atholl is a popular long-distance walk, but not the one I had in mind.

After Forest Lodge the glen narrows and becomes barer, with fine views back towards Bheinn a' Ghlo. At Dun Beag, a fairly recent Land Rover track has been bulldozed westwards to the Tarf, but I resisted its temptation and carried on north to the delightful Falls of Tarf and the Bedford Memorial Bridge. This bridge was built in 1885 to commemorate the death of an English student in Tarf Ford. It was erected by the Rights of Way Society, which had been formed after a celebrated case in 1847 against the Duke of Atholl which opened the glen to public access. This magical place is worth the extra couple of miles walk its visit entails, and was much admired by QueenVictoria, who forded it on horseback in 1861.

From the falls a good track leads, past ruined shielings, to a pony shelter high on the moor; I found it bereft of ponies, but full of frogs squirming profusely on the floor. I had been to the Tarf Hotel, as the Feith Uaine bothy is popularly called, a couple of times before, when it was semi-ruinous. Recently restored by the Mountain Bothies Association, it lies a bittock short of 2,000 ft, with little in the way of a path between it and the pony-hut, so I was very pleased to cross its portals about six hours out from Blair Atholl. Though obviously more used since restoration, the Tarf was empty when I arrived, and I passed the time reading the hut log book. Epic tales were there of people floundering in deep drifts and battling blizzards in winter, but most memorable was of a walker finding the rivers Tarf and Feithe Uaine joined in a loch, and of a six foot high wave of ice and water-melt crashing against the side of the 'Hotel'! I bedded at dusk, hoping for a good sleep and an early start next day, facing about the same distance but over immeasurably rougher terrain. Maybe I was mad, like a certain Robertson who escaped from a lunatic asylum in 1883, and made his home in the Tarf Bothy till captured?

The country around the Tarf is high rolling moorland, achieving its impact from loneliness and desolation rather than from dramatic grandeur. There can be few more 'empty quarters' in our islands. My plan was simple: to follow the waters of the Tarf to their head below Beinn Bhreac, and thence navigate a route through to Gaick. The sun struggled with mist on the tops as I set off, sticking close to the green sward at the riverside. This made pleasant going, occasionally helped by traces of animal-made paths. Landscape mirrored the sense of isolation: every hill was contoured like its neighbour and I thought this would be hard country to navigate in bad weather. The monotony was relieved by the chirping and bobbing of the dippers in the river, each pair of which seemed to inhabit its own particular stretch.

Apart from places where landslips on the banks forced river crossings, the going was easier than expected, till I reached the watershed and the river banks vanished in a mass of rutted peat hags and bogs. Here I encountered my first human artefact since the bothy: a line of cairns crossing the hags, apparently guiding the way to Beinn Bhreac, for what reason I could not imagine. The descent down the Allt a Chuil was rougher, picking up deer tracks now and again, the sides of the glen hemming me in. But visually it was a delight after the uniformity of the Tarf, as side rivulets created enticing glens and waterfalls to refresh the eye. Finally, at a couple of ruined shielings about a mile from the head of Glen Bruar, a track (definitely human-made) guided me down to a point where the old Minigaig pass (yet another of the so-called Mounth passes) dropped to Bruar. And I dropped down, for sustenance, four hours out from my 'Hotel'.

Gaick was still far off, and after lunch I was pleased to find a stalker's path leading off the Minigaig over the moorland above the Feith Ghorm Ailleag, a pleasant gorge with trees clinging to the waterfalls along its tributaries. The day was now clear and sunny, but this could be the most difficult part of the trek to navigate. The path ended at a group of butts, and in bad weather it would be so easy to continue along the burn which heads south into trackless territory. But a little nick in the steep banks at 8100.8050 is the key to unlock the route to Gaick. After some rough and tussocky hags, the Allt Garbh Ghaig began to descend out of the moors until—a bit further on than the O.S. map indicates—a reasonable path traces a route down. This glen is a little Dhu Kosi, steep and rocky above the tumbling burn.

Late afternoon brought hunger after my fasting in the wilderness, and also a rising wind, so I had eyes peeled for somewhere sheltered to light my primus when I saw a strange stilted structure ahead. On reaching it, I found it was surrounded by abandoned barbed wire and fence posts, and looked like a prison-camp tower. Had a Stalag film been shot here, or was it a proposed concentration camp for rights of way agitators? A ladder led between its legs, and I climbed up. Inside there was floor space and a seat, giving a fine view of the wind combing the hair of the waterfalls on Sron Bhuirich. Though it shoogled in the wind, I knew it would do—and for more than a kitchen, as I was uncertain of dossing possibilities further down-glen. The rest of the daylight hours, and those of night, were spent in hermit-like elevation.

On my coming out of the hills towards Gaick Lodge (a brilliant white against the ultramarine Loch an t-Seilich), the country changed dramatically into a model of glaciated landscape. Steep hills fell to huge verdant flats around the lodge. By it was a monument to the 'Loss of

Gaick', when four men were killed in an avalanche here in 1800—one of the victims was reputed to have had a pact with the devil. But the area was witness to a more diabolical tale of temptation hundreds of years before that. Walter Comyn was the feudal lord of Badenoch, and set off to supervise the building of a road through Gaick to Atholl, ordering that on his return all women between fifteen and thirty should be working naked in his fields. But he never returned to feast his eyes. His foot was found first, in the stirrup of his horse, which was maddened with terror and foaming at the mouth. Further searching revealed Walter's battered body with two eagles feasting on it...Until a century ago, a favourite curse of the old Badenoch people was 'Diol Bhaltair an Gaig ort!' ('Walter's fate in Gaick on you').

Hunger rather than lust was my problem, and I hoped to be spared Walter's fate as I faced the last, easier stage of my trek to Kingussie, down Glen Tromie. This glen reminded me of the Tilt, both in its wooded aspects, and the fact that it was traversed by a private estate road, with the occasional habitation. At Lynaberock stood a solitary ruin of a clachan that once had 200 people, a church and school. By Tromie Bridge I sat down, and ate my last few cold potatoes, hoping I looked pathetic enough to offer a lift to—and had success. I was so hungry, I feared I might hallucinate, and begin to see naked damsels in the Badenoch fields. But again luck was in, and I waited only five minutes for a train at Kingussie—sharing the platform with a giggle of girls, scented and dressed-up for a night in Inverness. But Walter's cruel fate kept all lascivious thoughts at bay. On board I committed a deadly sin, but not Lust. Gluttony triumphed as I stuffed myself in the buffet, after two days sparse fare.

I had thoughts that this trek was a 'first', but later found I had been beaten to it—by Walter's mad horse. After his death in Gaick—by witchcraft, avalanche or at the hands of outraged husbands—his horse had dragged him to the Ghaig headwaters and left him there minus his foot. It then careered to the vicinity of the Tarf Falls, where it was found—with foot—at a place still called Ruigh Leth-chois (shieling of the one foot). The mad beast had found the Atholl High Route as logical a one as I had, if not as enjoyable.

Echo:
The Minigaig and Access: History Repeated

Shortly before my tramp to Gaick, the Duke of Atholl, one of Britain's largest and richest landowners, had conceded the right of way on the Minigaig Pass from Calvine to Kingussie. His Lordship had argued that hikers were upsetting the shoot. Since the thirteenth century the 'Comyn's Road'—as it was formerly known—over the Grampian mountains has been used by armies, drovers and walkers. After opposition from Perth and Kinross District Council, representations by the Rights of Way Society and the threat of a mass trespass, the Duke backed down from his attempts to deny access. Even when the unspeakable are pursuing the eatable, passage by the Minigaig cannot be barred, although wandering off the route may lead to the possibility of a charge of 'aggravated trespass'.

History has here repeated itself, since a previous Duke ofAtholl, as mentioned in the last chapter, tried to close the road from Blair Atholl to Braemar via Glen Tilt in 1847. A group of Edinburgh botanists—led by Professor Balfour, out collecting scientific specimens—clashed with the Duke's ghillies, giving rise to the humorous lines of the 'Ballad of Glen Tilt':

> Balfour had a mind as weel
> As ony Duke could hae, man:
> Quo' he 'There's ne'er a kilted chiel
> Shall drive us back this day, man.
> It's justice and it's public richt
> We'll pass Glen Tilt afore the nicht.'

The 'Battle of Glen Tilt' went to law, and the Duke lost the access litigation, raised by the forerunners of the present Rights of Way Society, and supported by the Town Council of Perth, whose Provost the Duke had assaulted.

The Duke fought a reargard action, occasionally molesting walkers, and reputedly destroying a bridge over the River Tarf to limit access. The Rights of Way Society responded by funding the building of the

Bedford Memorial Bridge which—much repaired—still stands as a relic of the case.

The whole struggle for rights of way in Scotland has a particular connection with the region of the Grampian hills and glens. In the 1880s Duncan MacPherson tried to forbid access to Glen Doll, forcibly restricting entry. The Rights of Way Society fought him through the courts, appeal courts and House of Lords, at a cost of £650, to establish the right of way. But other glens were closed, and James Bryce stated in the years before the First World War that, 'it is hardly possible to stir off the roads in the neighbourhood of Braemar without being confronted by a ghillie and threatened with proceedings by interdict.'

Although not a native Aberdonian, Bryce had a long connection with the city, being Liberal MP for Aberdeen South from 1885 to 1906, and President of the Cairngorm Club for 32 years. The Scottish hills were his first love, but he mountaineered widely, climbing Mount Ararat , the Vignemale in the Pyrenees, Hekla in Iceland, and having Mount Bryce in the Canadian Rockies named after him. His political career eventually saw him appointed Ambassador to the USA from 1906 to 1913.

On behalf of mountaineers, Bryce made several (unsuccessful) attempts to have his 'Access to Moors and Mountains Bill' passed in the House of Commons. Because of its radicalism, many in the Cairngorm Club dissociated themselves from Bryce's actions. For his Bill would have established a general right to roam. He stated with typical vigorousness:

> We are by no means content to be kept to a specified, limited path in the centre of a mountain. If, for instance, I were going to the top of a mountain and saw in the distance cliffs overhanging a loch, I am not to be prevented from going to that loch because it happens to be in a deer forest and off the footpath.

The failure of Bryce's Bill is one of the—in fact probably the greatest —lost opportunities on mountain access.

In the 1920s the Mounth road over Mount Keen in Glen Tanar was closed by the Trustees of the Baron of Glentanar. The *Aberdeen Free Press* reported that 'great gates are shut at night, while further up the glen there are two other sets of gates…intended to bar the way to Mount Keen.' The Rights of Way Society persuaded the Aberdeen County Council to put up funds to fight the case, which again was won in 1930, establishing the right of way. For a half century after this, there was very little willingness on the part of Scottish landlords to challenge the de facto 'right to roam' which gradually emerged in the inter-war period. Today, however, the dangers of the re-emergence of a pre-1914 situation are real.

While many landowners would be content to see governments of whatever political stripe give them financial compensation for 'managing' the countryside and 'allowing' access, or for 'not developing' sites of scenic or scientific interest, there is also a general spread of resistance to unlimited access to the hills. In thirty years of hill-going I have never seen so many PRIVATE or NO ENTRY signs, or signs limiting access to the periods when culling or lambing—which can extend to half the year—are not taking place.

Previously, such signs could be treated with contempt, since the trespass law in Scotland made only attendant damage committed a criminal offence. As a man who was not a firebrand, but a Conservative party member and Special Constable in the General Strike of 1926 (the Rev. A.E. Robertson), said,

> Simple trespass in Scotland is not a criminal offence. The sign TRESPASS-ERS WILL BE PROSECUTED is an empty threat. What the owner of the ground can do is to proceed against you in the civil courts. He cannot lay violent hands upon you.

But the new crime of 'aggravated trespass' makes such a view outdated. Interfering with legitimate activity of a landowner, e.g. walking off a right of way during shooting, lambing or any other 'legitimate' activity, now becomes a crime. Landowners would no doubt defend such activities, as providing 'income' and 'employment'. Firstly it should be pointed out that their custodianship of Scottish mountain land has turned it into an ecological desert. And secondly, it is time the far greater boosts to income and employment, provided by walkers and mountaineers in rural areas through spending on food, petrol, accommodation etc, were considered in the access debate.

It is not enough to resist controls on access: outdoor enthusiasts should be campaigning for a legally enshrined Right of Access, as was fought for by James Bryce. Supporters of such a policy would point to the Scandinavian example, with the 'allemansrat' and freedom to roam. Without the scourge of landlordism, the upland areas of Norway are an environmental paradise compared to Scotland.

It may well be that history is about to repeat itself, with attempts made to control or limit access to the hills on grounds of profit, or a pseudo-concern for conservation—and assisted by the invention of the offence of 'aggravated trespass'. This has to be resisted in all ways, but the ultimate defence of the freedom to roam is—just do it! Let us leave the last word to Professor Balfour:

> For Dukes shall we
> Care a'e bawbee?
> The road's as free
> To you and me
> As to his Grace himsel, man.

October:
OCTOBER COUNTRY

Often, at the end of the stag-shooting season in mid-October, one can snatch days that are almost summer-like in their wondrousness, the last such of the year. The sun can be as hot, though more briefly, as on a summer's day. However the colours on the moors and woods have turned, and the smells raised by the unseasonal warmth are of damp earth and rotting vegetation, not the fresher ones of summer. We were lucky, the kid and I, that we had managed to poach just such a spell of weather for his first trip to Bob Scott's—the new one. He was getting a big lad now, with his first pair of Scarpa Vibrams, his first mountain-bike trip to a bothy, and hopefully, if the weather held, his first 4,000-er on the morrow.

In half an hour we had made the bothy on the bikes. It stayed warm in the late afternoon: but the temperature fell as the stars came out, and that night we had a frost. We shared the bothy only with a crackling fire which drove away the chill. The kid gave me a wee ceilidh on his chanter, and as I listened to the music and watched the fire, I recognised one of the tunes that Mac had used to sing a song to—'The Poacher of Braemar'.

'Tell me about it,' he asked (no longer was it 'sing it to me').

It was the usual tale, from the period of the full ferocity of the game laws in the first half of the nineteenth century. The poacher vowed never to stop or be trapped, enjoying the excitement as much as the income from his trade.

One day I went to Bheinn a Bhuird my gun intae my hand
Soon there follaed after me six keepers in a band
They swore they would lay hands on me but I soon let them know
I am the roving Highlander could prove their overthrow.

But like hundreds, thousands, before and after him, he was eventually caught and transported to Van Diemen's Land. The barbarities of this era, with its man-traps and dog-packs, often leading to shoot-outs with gamekeepers, gradually eased as punishment for poaching declined. But even around 1900, in the northern edges of the Cairngorms, a poacher, pursued by a posse of police and gamekeepers, shot one of them dead.

'Have you ever been poaching?' the kid enquired.

Sadly, I had to answer no. For despite my desire to combine my atavistic impulses with my hatred of landlordism, I had never had the opportunity. It still went on. Mac had a pal who when asked, after gifting some venison to a friend, where he had got it, would reply, 'Between the eyes'. He was famous for his open-pit barbecues. Davie told me of mates of his who were presented with wrapped venison when in a nameless bothy by 'hunters home from the hill'. Too intimidated to refuse it, when they hitched a lift home next day, they left enough blood in the back seat of the obliging car to raise a cry of murder. My participation was limited to being an accessory. Whenever we visited Lewis we would come home laden with salmon tasting all the sweeter for not being paid for. And there too, guns were still used. On one trip we heard of a salmon bailiff who shot at, and hit, an escaping poacher's car. Astonishingly, the bailiff was only admonished, the local sheriff presumably not knowing that poaching was no longer a capital offence.

Next day was a lucky thirteenth. A couple of tents had arrived during the night, and the rime was still glistening on them when I stepped outside. But the clearness of the sky promised warmth later. We hastened away, disturbing some red squirrels outside Derry Lodge at their preparations for winter. Once we were on the sandy path up Glen Luibeg it was warm enough to be summer, an illusion conspired at by the evergreen of the pines against the sky. Though the woodland was generally badly maintained, I was pleased further on to find a stand of pinewoods fenced for protection, and given areas of empty moor to recolonise as well. I have seen claims that there were not really all that many more forested areas in the Highlands a hundred years ago: maybe so, for by then the damage had been done. But John Taylor, the Water Poet, visiting these mountains in 1618, observed that the 'Earle of Marr' had

as many firre trees…as would serve for masts (from this time to the end of the worlde) for all the shippes, carackes, hoyes, galleys, boates, barkes and water-crafts that are now, or can be in the worlde…

The path up Glen Luibeg gave us no problem, but the crossing of the burn itself, to gain Sron Riach, did: from the melt of early snow-falls it was in semi-spate. Once up Sron Riach and onto the plateau, we were into the snow, silly soft stuff that would not last long, but which gave the hills a fine honing, sharpened them against the blue sky. On the still, clear summit we sunbathed, eyes pulled towards the Cairn Toul/Braeriach massif, below which the green sward of Corrour Bothy was visible. For all the world, the Lairig Ghru could have been the pass from Spiterstulen to Leirvassbu I had tramped in the Jotunheim that summer, Cairn Toul a mirror of Styggeho, MacDhui itself Gald-hoppigen...

We had seen no-one, nothing that moved, since the squirrels. Not even a deer.

We picked our way down the Macdhui boulder-field, a long slow work, and at the col met our first fellows: a couple of lads out from Corrour, with the boulders to ascend, a gruelling task. We on the other hand had the delight of the ridge of Carn a' Mhaim, hardly a Cuillin, but for the Cairngorms a wee gem. Rested again on the summit, getting a bit tired now, before the descent to the Luibeg Bridge and the long walk back to the bothy. Though a wind had got up, it was still clear and sunny. In the trees around the bothy, down in the haugh by the river, it was already cool. Despite his tiredness, I forced the boy to collect wood while I made the meal: it would soon be cold, and too dark to go faggot collecting.

That evening we had company. Over our food, a young English geologist came in from one of the tents outside to prepare his meal. Some harmless remark made by the geologist about a future ice-age led to he and my son having a heated exchange about the burning out of the sun and other matters. The geologist clearly lost interest in the debate before his antagonist did.

'Dinna deave the mannie,' I insisted, but none too earnestly.

It was good to get a break, have a few drams...and I gave the geologist a couple for his trouble.

He left, and as I worked my way down the bottle, the boy worked his way through his chanter repertoire. This brought in another visitor from the other tent, a lassie who had just traversed a Cairngorm Pass—I forget which—on her own, and who claimed to be a piper herself. My boy (at the age when lassies can't do *anything* right) expressed scepticism, and an exchange of tunes took place between the two of them that kept us, with what was left of the whisky, going for some time. She praised him, but he was worsted in the competition.

'How many Munros have you done?' he tried—but here too the answer (more than he had) gave him little satisfaction. He had to remain content with his first 4,000-er.

It was dull and with a spitting of rain on the cycle out next day. Half way back there are huge green areas, rickled with low dykes, where formerly the inhabitants of the glen lived. Clearances here were early. The Earl of Mar's brother wrote in 1726 to his factor, 'As to Glenluy...we desire you to eject those people after their harvest is over...and the more you have along with you there will be the less opposition.'

When we left the flats were occupied by several hundred half-wild deer. How easy it would be, I thought, on an estate now with no resident gamekeeper, to kill some of these semi-domesticated animals. We resumed our cycle to the Derry Gates.

Back for refreshments in Braemar, a town that had hardly changed in appearance in thirty years. A Sleepytoon. And then home. We had successfully poached the trip from the imminence of winter.

Echo:
Guarding Old Derry's Gates: a Century of Luibeg Keepers

To many climbers the Derry gates near the Linn o' Dee, leading to the Mar Lodge estate and the central Cairngorms, are on a par with the Pearly Gates. Once, entry here was jealously guarded and only the elect—as in the Calvinist vision of heaven—were admitted. But in the twentieth century this earthly paradise for mountaineers has become democratised. Today the estate is uninhabited. But for a century until 1977 it supported resident keepers—the St Peters of the Derry Gates.

In contrast to most other areas in the Highlands, Upper Deeside was cleared of its inhabitants for deer, not for sheep, creating huge sporting estates virtually devoid of people. The Lodge was built for the shooting in the mid-nineteenth century by the Duke of Fife, with a keeper's cottage half a mile away at Luibeg. Poaching remained a problem, and a watcher's bothy was built at Corrour in the Lairig Ghru in 1877. Here a keeper would spend the summer months, up from Luibeg.

One of the first keepers, if not the first, was Charlie Robertson. Like many on Upper Deeside at this time he was fluently bilingual in Gaelic and Doric, and his local knowledge of place-names and lore allowed him to correct many of the mistakes in the original O.S. survey of the area. In the 80s and 90s the Cairngorms were still quiet. Although the Cairngorm Club had been founded in 1889, it originally ran but three excursions a year, generally using hotel accommodation. Thus the odd walker, like the naturalist Seton Gordon who visited Robertson, must have done much to relieve the loneliness of his stay from June till October at the bothy below the Devil's Point. Charlie Robertson also passed the time by searching for Cairngorm stones; and taming the bothy mice, which would perch on his boots, begging for cheese.

Seton Gordon also knew Robertson's successor, John Mackintosh, known as the Piper. The naturalist—no mean piper himself—used to share impromptu ceilidhs with the watcher by the peat fire of a night. On one occasion their combined talents caused a herd of deer to descend from Cairn Toul, and to dance on their hind legs to the music. Mackintosh was a fund of local lore, and one of the many stories Seton Gordon learned from him was that concerning the Tree of Gold— Craobh an Oir—in Glen Luibeg where a cateran is reported to have buried a hoard of treasure. Mackintosh too was a Gaelic speaker, and when his children went down to the school at Inverey, they had no English.

The last occupant of Corrour was Charlie Grant, who welcomed travellers with whisky and tales. Charlie would leave the bothy for Braemar at the week-end to attend chapel—often fording the Dee waist-high en route. Behind him he would leave the door open for any traveller to use the bothy, with its armchair and box bed.

Welcoming as these keepers were at Corrour, they had to present another face at other times, especially when the gentry were in attendance at the shooting. The Duke of Fife had an unenviable record of attempting to deny access, threatening mountaineers with prosecution and even pressurising local tenants to refuse to take in summer visitors. Then, as today, the 'gamie' was a different creature when the laird was around!

As early as 1878, Alexander Copland, later a founder member of the Cairngorm Club, complained in the *Aberdeen Journal* about 'Our native Mumbo Jumbos who molest the traveller in Glen Derry, Glen Luibeg and other wilds...selfishly, out of excessive zeal for shooting deer...'

These 'Mumbo Jumbos' mentioned were undoubtedly the same Robertsons and Mackintoshes who were so hospitable when the laird was away—or when his back was turned!

World War I was to have a major impact, causing a crisis in the great estates which affected Mar also. Corrour was never occupied nor maintained after 1914, and the number of estate keepers was reduced. As a revenue-raising measure, the estate even allowed cars to drive to Derry Lodge on payment of a toll: this was unthinkable pre-1914.

Also, the landowner had to learn to live with the increase in the numbers of mountaineers. Corrour, which hardly knew a visitor pre-1914, recorded a staggering total of 2,000 overnights between 1928 and 1933! In addition, the Rights of Way Society was very active, and landowners faced expensive litigation if they wished to attempt access restrictions.

There were several stalkers at Luibeg after 1918, including Sandy MacDonald who heard a Zeppelin passing over the Cairngorms in 1916, and found a flare it had dropped in 1921. MacDonald was known as Sandy Bynack, as he had ghillied at Bynack Lodge near the Chest of Dee, before moving to Luibeg with his family in 1912. One of his daughters, Nell, supplemented the family income by guiding tourists from Braemar up Ben Macdhui. That could have been a sackable offense before 1914.

By the late 1920s, Alexander Grant was in occupation at Luibeg, and his position passed to his son Ian in 1934. At New Year 1928 both father and son were involved in the unavailing attempt to rescue Glasgow walkers Baird and Barrie, who had taken in the New Year at Corrour Bothy, and were later found dead in Glen Einich. In atrocious conditions they battled to within a quarter mile of Corrour, and turned back. Ian Grant, who wore the kilt even on rescues, observed,

I never faced a worse blizzard. My father's moustache was frozen and part of his face coated with ice...We...never caught a glimpse of the bothy...

Ian was a fitness enthusiast, and had a weight-lifting gym in a Luibeg outhouse! Affleck Grey was a close friend and often crossed the hills to ceilidh with the Grants. He recalls that Gaelic was still widely used at Luibeg, but it was probably not the first language any more, since Ian partly taught himself from books.

Ghillies were becoming regular participants in mountain rescue. Ian Grant led a party composed of local gamekeepers and policemen in the search for the body of Norman Macleod of Aberdeen, who died on Ben MacDhui in 1934. Macleod had camped at Derry Lodge and left his tent there. Toleration of camping at such a spot indicated that a

Bob Scott with 'Punchie', Luibeg Cottage in the background

more liberal attitude was now taken to access. This was to broaden out even further, with the arrival after World War II of Luibeg's most famous and longest resident keeper, Bob Scott.

Although Scott's father had ghillied on the Mar estate for thirty years, Bob only took up residency at Luibeg in his forties. Previously he had worked for the County Council and served during the War in the 8th Army. His residency coincided with another explosion of mountaineering activity and increased ease of access. Derry Lodge, which the estate no longer utilised, was leased to the Cairngorm Club in 1951, and in that palace of twelve rooms, with lounge, drying room, kitchen, bathroom and heating, took place the—as it seemed to the 'scruffs' passing—rather genteel meets of the Cairngorm Club. But then those who passed were heading for what they regarded as a better place—Bob Scott's Bothy!

After taking occupation of Luibeg, Scott opened various outbuildings as bothy accommodation for mountaineers. The main one was an old wooden building with a fireplace which had presumably been a ghillies' day bothy, with stable and woodshed attached. For thirty years this housed the anarchic vagabonds who mountaineered in the Cairngorms—and whose company Scott loved. One of the earliest to use the bothy was the great Aberdeen mountaineer Tom Patey, who recalls that at Hogmanay in 1948 there were forty climbers in the howff with its roaring fire, and that he was relegated to the woodshed, where the snow was drifting and the thermometer recorded forty degrees of frost.

Scott could at first sight appear intimidating, with his eternal plusfours, deerstalker and booming voice. Bob was the first Luibeg keeper 'without the Gaelic', and his tongue was of the richest, broadest Doric, which he refused to compromise whoever the listener, and in which he delivered his judgements and opinions in an ungainsayable way. He was also a stern disciplinarian, imposing bothy rules ruthlessly. I bet Patey had to pay, even for the woodshed—for the canny Scott charged a shilling a night for the use of his bothy, raising it, I recall, to 10p on decimalisation.

Tales of Scott—and told by Scott when he deigned to converse with the bothy inmates—are legion. A regular visitor to Luibeg in the 1950s was the Dundonian, Syd Scroggie, who had been blinded at the end of the War. When Scroggie and a friend indicated their intention to head further, Scott replied with typical bluntness, 'There's been widden legs here afore, but never a blind bugger awa tae Corrour that I mind o'. (Corrour had been restored by the Cairngorm Club in 1950.) Scroggie's book, *The Cairngorms Scene*, tells many stories about Scott, and the walkers whose lives were saved by the existence of his bothy, and by Bob's help. On one occasion a vast mountain rescue was mounted by the RAF, and a climber brought to Luibeg. Scott was refreshingly forthright in his account.

'There was nae need for a' the stushy ava. If someone hid jist telt us he was a diabetic, jist the ae lad carrying a peel wad hae been a that wis wantit.'

But Scott was also a fervent defender of his employers' rights, guarding against vandalism and poaching. Once some ingenuous fishermen approached him and asked if there was anywhere they could fish. He replied, deadpan, 'Only Loch Avon—and that's nae in my beat', before bursting, as he was wont to do, into gales of laughter at his own humour.

Scott retired from Luibeg in 1977, a hundred years after Corrour, its abandoned outpost, was built. Today Luibeg too lies empty. His bothy, free now, continued to be used, but sadly was burnt down in the mid 80s. However, such was the respect and affection that Scott was held in by north-east mountaineers, that a fair replica of the bothy has been built close by and named in his honour: Bob Scott's Bothy.

The Mar estate itself went through various metamorphoses, before ending up in the hands of a mega-rich American whose wife, apparently, wanted to be the Queen's neighbour! But a constant factor has been the steady deterioration of the land: loss of tree-cover without natural regeneration, erosion of the soil due to over-grazing by deer, not to mention the obscene bulldozing of a land-rover track far into Glen Derry. The sad ruins of Derry Lodge symbolise the estate's plight.

The recent purchase of the estate by the National Trust allows us to hope that Derry will now be run in the public interest, not for landed privilege. And to hope that we might one day see a keeper back in Luibeg with an environmentalist remit, promoting regeneration and facilitating responsible access. But if that ever happened, he or she would have a hard act to follow.

November:
GUY FAWKES NIGHT

The Annual General Wet Weekend was upon us again, and I had organised a trip to the 'Gorms. Despite the fact it was my third return to
my native heath in a year, I felt guiltless of regressive mania and pointed
out that Corndavon—our destination—had never been graced with my
presence before, was probably the only bothy in the only part of the
'Gorms I had never been to. We would take some fireworks, have a
bonfire—and were sure we would have the place to ourselves in that
dead season of early November.

I had done a few trips alone over summer, taken away the Bash
Street Kids, even been away with my wife…I fancied a Big Boy week-
end for a change, as I told the Lad in the car as we drove northwards.
Drinking, Talking Dirty, Being Untidy, Scratching and Farting…

'You mean, the way women behave?' he asked—and he spent the
time till Blairgowrie, where we met the Mafia and Mr 10%, telling me
of when he was a musician, and did the annual trip to Blairgowrie at
the berry picking, when it was like Dawson at the Gold Rush, tinker
women fighting over a man, or a pair of knickers, or something else
equally worthless, and of the unsolicited advances he had to reject continually, from drunken, would-be groupies. We arrived at Blair. But as
we ate our splendid fish supper, the place was as quiet as the grave.
Mind you, I told the company, it was the last place I had ever been
wolf-whistled, which probably said something about its womenfolk.

The fish supper had given us a drouth, so we halted for a couple of
pints at the Fife in Braemar, before heading off up Glen Gairn, scan-
ning the map for the land-rover turn off to Corndavon. But there was
no need for a map, there were already half a dozen cars there, and we
squeezed our own two beside them with difficulty. It was a muggy
walk in on an overcast night, but easy to find the way and in about an
hour we knew we were near the bothy. I was a little concerned that it
might be full, given the number of cars. However, double, triple the
number could not have filled it with their occupants.

Corndavon Lodge had been palatial. At a safe distance away from it were the servant and animal quarters, together. An architectural paradigm of Victorian class consciousness. But these quarters, across a dividing burn, now provide the most magnificent bothy accommodation in Scotland. Firstly, it is huge, with a warren of rooms which sheltered sixty people on that trip, and could have sheltered double that. In the rooms were bunks, settees, and fireplaces—one room even had a functioning range from whose bubbling kettle we were given a friendly cup of tea when we arrived. There was a septic tank toilet in the ruins of one out-building, and all the rubbish was carried out in bins by the lads who maintained it, members of the Grampian Transport Group M.C.

We had a splendid welcome from these lads, and from their wives and children with whom they had come with intent to celebrate Guy Fawkes the next day: I quickly realised this might mean we could do a big hill day and not worry about collecting wood. Apart from our crew and a couple of English lads biking, everyone was 'fae Aibirdeen', and belied in their warmth and generosity all the stereotypes about Aberdonians which I previously have felt it is my single-handed duty to refute in my own personal behaviour. By the end of the weekend, Erchie was 'fit-ing' and 'foo-ing' with the best of them.

We shared a room with the English cyclists. Now, as everyone knows, I have nothing against the English. The real test of a Scotsman's credo, 'A man's a man for a' that', lies in whether he extends it to Englishmen, and I do. But at times they sorely test you. Often they will sit autistically in a bothy—maybe its the freeze-dried food they eat. At other, inappropriate times they will talk all night, as these ones did. About the maintenance of mountain bikes. I got up and moved through to a room full of shaggy dogs and Aberdonians, it was that bad.

Morning brought low cloud. Mr 10% wasn't feeling too good, and fancied doing a Corbett.

'That'll make you feel worse,' I suggested.

But he and the Mafia went off to trundle through the bogs of Broon Coo Hill, as it is kent in these airts, for the good of their souls, promising to absolve the Lad and me from wood-duty. For we had a big day planned. Probably rather ambitious for that time of year in retrospect.

The Lad had started ticking late, with the result that he and my boy were constantly leap-frogging each other in the Munros League Tables: at present the Lad was one behind. Now, I felt paternal pride should not impair my objectivity, so I thought we might do Ben Avon, the great whaleback with its mighty tors, like molluscan encrustations on a back of blubber-moss, and be back for the party. The Lad concurred, and we set off for the ruins of Loch Builg Lodge, he trusting in my navigational skills, and paying his dues by listening to all my old boring Cairngorm stories. Occasionally I gave him a test:

'Have I told you the story about the Loch Builg Boat House?'

'No', he replied.

'But it's in that book I gave you, a personal signed copy. Have ye nae read it?'

'Oh, THAT story, I thought you meant another one,' he then smiled, almost credibly. You can see why he has gone far in social work management.

A path was marked towards Carn Drochaid, but we never found it till we stumbled on its virtual end, below where the ground steepened towards the massif of Ben Avon. By that time we were rising into the falling, dripping mist. We found a cairn which I could identify from the map, and then took a bearing for Clach Choutsaich, the first of the granite tors on the huge inverted V-shaped summit plateau of our mountain. We walked on, seeing only each other, until a massive petrified monster loomed over us as if frozen in aggression. We scrambled up its sides, despite the dripping cold, the Lad amazed at the stone excrescence.

Points on the map followed each other: 3625, 3662, 3649; each a massive, inert mastodon, discovered by the tiniest flickering of a needle. Each we scrambled up, over and round, until only the last tor lay ahead of us, Leabaidh an Daimh Bhuidhe, a name so fine it arouses an interest in place-names even in me: Bed of the Yellow Stag. Taking my bearings I called to the Lad, 'One to go, at that's the summit.'

Arrived, we scrambled awhile over the extensive top, where the remains of earlier snow falls filled deep cracks. I wished for the sky to clear, so my companion could see Garbh Choire and the Mitre Ridge, one of the finest mountainscapes in Scotland. We waited in vain till cold sent us back, reversing our compass-bearings but giving the mastodons a wide berth this time. Just in case they woke up.

I was really pleased with my navigation, really pleased. And maybe it was my over-elaborate pedantic explanation to the Lad of how I had done it that was my downfall. We missed point 3625. Even though it was only by a whisker, it put us on a wrong course. Instead of getting back to Loch Builg, we dropped down the Allt and Eas Mhor, a tussocky, frustrating descent, to the upper reaches of Glen Gairn, where we regained the track.

Now this glen's higher parts are amongst the wildest and most remote in the Cairngorms, so they tell me. But I was tired: we had done a dozen or more miles already and the night would not be long in falling from the sky. We had a full six miles back to Corndavon. We tried to be cheery, pass comment on the landscape, make conversation. And for a couple of miles were quite successful. But in the dark of a late November afternoon,the only things that interest you are food, warmth and rest. Since we could have none of them, we fell silent, gritted teeth and marched on, heads down. I feel I did not do Glen Gairn justice: maybe I'll go back sometime.

We saw the fire from far off: the fireworks were beginning when we arrived. So we made our meal, and ate it outside with the company. Our friends had collected wood, and we donated our fireworks to someone who had taken charge, and went to get our whisky. Children ran about, wide-eyed, and watched the explosions tracing the sky. Around the fire there was conviviality and tale-swapping, while, in odd corners of the bothy, wee ceilidhs were going on. Erchie, as ever, was a star attraction with his songs, and did not get to bed till 5 a.m., by which time I'm sure, if they could, the G.T.G.M.C. would have made him a freeman of Aberdeen. But nine hours and at least double that of miles on Ben Avon sent the Lad and me to a more respectable bedding-down. Followed by a sleep so sound, we never even heard the later celebrations.

These celebrations were a well-behaved family occasion. Husbands, wives and children round the fire, songs and banter in the bothy. There was copious drink, and a couple of lads sat quietly in a recess room smoking 'the weed'. No one misbehaved, no-one annoyed anyone else, and no damage was done. Yet I was later to hear that this and other similar occasions were the excuse used by the new estate management of Invercauld to close Corndavon on the grounds of 'drink and drugs parties'. For there is another agenda here: this new management intends to make the estate pay, and thinks clearing out scruff who might disturb the deer is one method. Additionally, they find themselves in sole possession of a bothy rebuilt and maintained by those now barred its use! Once again we are held hostage to the whims of landlordism.

On the walk out it came to me that, almost by accident, we were celebrating festivals in our trips more and more: indulging in ritual and tradition. I mentioned this to Erchie, who remarked,

'Well, whit is there after yer Munros? Except for Corbetts?'

I suppose that is true: maybe ritual is another unavailing protection against the dying of the light. Anyway, it was then that I had an idea, asking Erchie,

'Whit state is yer "Tam o' Shanter" in, Erchie?'

It was when he assured me it was a bit rusty, but still serviceable, that I felt we might have another ritual in the offing, in January. You need a compass, a flickering pointer, to keep you going when the mist starts to fall.

Echo:
The Other Queen of Royal Deeside: Maggie Gruer

Coming down Glen Gairn from Corndavon, you look over Balmoral and the lands of 'Royal' Deeside. We passed it at a time when the King-to-be and his aspirant Queen were doing more than all my youthful anarchist activities to spread republican feeling. I wondered if the 'auld Queen' would have been amused by their doings. What is, ultimately, nobility of spirit? Here, I think, is an example.

While everyone knows of the original Deeside Queen—Victoria— another who was in part her contemporary and was named the 'Queen of the Cairngorm Passes' by her admirers, deserves wider recognition. While Prime Ministers and foreign monarchs visited Balmoral, mountaineers visiting Maggie Gruer's Thistle Cottage in Inverey spoke with at least equal fervour about the delights of their stay.

It is now hard to imagine the Scottish hills without the range of Youth Hostels, club huts and mountain bothies which provide basic accommodation for mountaineers. But before the First World War, and long after, when the hills were more densely peopled than now, the only refuge apart from expensive hotels was in the homes of game-keepers and crofters, many of them glad of the company—and income—provided by the mountaineers. Such a system provided shelter at Thistle Cottage with the Gruers, in the remote Aberdeenshire hamlet of Inverey, for half a century.

The Gruers, like many of the inhabitants of Inverey, had been cleared from Glen Ey to make way for the increasingly lucrative sport of deer-stalking in the mid-nineteenth century. Despite a slow population decline, by the time the mountaineers arrived around 1880 there were still about 100 people in the clachan, mainly crofters. Though there was a school, the predominant language was still Gaelic. When Maggie

Gruer was born in 1862, it was only 40 years since the last active survivor of the Jacobite rebellion had died on upper Deeside!

Thistle Cottage was very much a subsistence crofter-holding. Like many others, Maggie's mother and father took in climbers, especially from the newly-formed Cairngorm Club after 1889; but when her parents died Maggie, who remained unmarried, seems to have expanded the concern and made it her main occupation, and doubtless a source of income. The bed and breakfast accommodation provided was basic. Up to forty people would find space on the floor of the sitting room of the cottage, or in the byre along with her cow. If further space were needed, a later arrival might be told, 'Ye can hae a shak-doon at the tap o the stair!' Maggie supposedly favoured her male guests over the female: in any event the accommodation was sex-segregated. Ben Humble tells of asking to sleep in her barn, but Maggie replied, 'Na, na. I hae twa bonnie lassies in there and ye'll no get in there.' (Although a native Gaelic speaker, Maggie seems to have been equally fluent in the Doric, which had all but eliminated Gaelic on upper Deeside by her death in 1939.)

But her guests needed have no fear of starvation. One visitor describes arriving and being force-fed home-made scones, butter, oatcakes, cranberry jam and eggs from her own hens. Maggie's scones were particularly famous, and in this she was following her mother: apparently Gladstone, when out on one of his massive Cairngorm hikes, would always call in at Thistle Cottage for a bag, on his way back to Balmoral. One wonders if Victoria was amused, especially as he was often late for dinner.

Maggie provided entertainment as well as food and lodgings. She held dances in her barn, with fiddle accompaniment, and she herself joined in the fun. Entrance, with midnight tea, was 3d. Visitors tell that whisky was not in short supply. Maggie herself was a great raconteur at these gatherings. Tales of Gladstone were mingled with those about the Earl of Fife and Mar Lodge, and of Queen Victoria and John Brown. She was clearly not overawed by royalty, and used to tell a story about how she had 'walloped the royal dog' when she found it worrying her calf. Nor was she in awe of the landed class, whom she described as 'chappies wha put up the boardies wi them screedies, "Not to look at the grouse"'. This independence of spirit was to find a suitable outlet.

The slow death of crofting in Inverey made tourist income for such as Maggie ever more important. But the local hunting interest attempted to prevent their tenants from taking visitors in the summer and shooting seasons. Maggie led the resistance, organising a campaign of letter-writing to the press, and to Parliament, leading to capitulation

Maggie Gruer, with her famous teapot, outside Thistle Cottage

by the Duke of Fife and other local lairds like Farquharson of Invercauld. 'I held my head fu' high,' she told Janet Adam Smith, 'I was aye proud.' The local lairds now seemed to see Maggie as worthy of attention, as she indicated: 'But we're chief now, and it's "How are you today Miss Gruer?"—and the car sent up for me at the election to vote for the Tories. I tak the car, but…' Her political sympathies are probably indicated by the fact the one of her cats was called Ramsay MacDonald, after the first Labour Prime Minister.

Maggie was not herself a hill-woman, and apparently her knowledge of the land beyond Inverey, which she freely imparted, was vague and awe-inspiring. This possibly prompted the comment of one wit in her visitors' book—which she insisted everyone sign after eating the compulsory breakfast of porridge and eggs,

> If I perish in the Pass
> At least I'll perish knowing
> That when I died I had inside
> The nicest breakfast going.

Other visitors noted in her guest-book were the Rev A. E. Robertson, first man to complete his 'Munros'—and the son of Hugh Munro himself. Baron and Baroness Kress of Nürnberg were there, as was Henry Alexander, Provost of Aberdeen and author of the original SMC *Cairngorm Guide*. In the democratised inter-war years, Cycling Clubs, Boy Scout Clubs, the Rucksack Club and even a Vegetarian Society found shelter with her. The Cairngorm Club's members, some of whom first-footed Maggie every Hogmanay, were among the most frequent visitors. Many wrote entries in Maggie's adoptive Doric:

> Here's tae Maggie Gruer
> O some tea ye can be sure
> Ah cannae write nae mair
> My airms and legs are awfu sair.

Maggie continued to run her concern till her death in Thistle Cottage in 1939, after which her Visitors' Books and chair were donated to the Cairngorm Club. Inverey's relentless decline continued: the school closed after the war when only half a dozen families remained. Today there are a few holiday homes, a Youth Hostel, and a hut of the Cairngorm Club. And reading the accounts of those who visited the 'Queen of the Cairngorm Passes', a person of natural nobility, we can only envy their good fortune in attendance at her court.

December:
A GUID NEW YEAR

When younger, I used to spend a good part of the festive season bothying. We would go away just after Christmas, and often take in New Year at a doss, free from parental monitoring. City traditions of Hogmanay are weakening, so we decided to take in the New Year once again at a bothy, the Monklands Mafiosi and I. We would have the lot: lumps of coal, black bun, whisky...and a tall dark handsome stranger, most of which description I flattered myself I fitted.

'Most?' queried the Dominie pointedly.

'Well, I'm nae exactly a stranger, am I?' was the reply.

It was decided to go to Slugain Howff, which it had been a long-held ambition of the Mafiosi to view, a bit like the Grand Canyon, Niagara Falls, and other wonders of the world. In addition, I had been there in summer with the boy, and noticed it was in much need of repair: especially the door, which was hanging on its hinges. Now, I had just done a major bathroom renovation, and there was plenty of nice pine wood left over—with the purchase of a couple of stout hinges and a sneck, we would do the repairs, put something back into the hills for what we took out. A noble aim.

'And besides,' I pointed out, 'we can work a flanker wi the gamie, if we tell him we'll be daein the repairs. We'll get tae drive the car a couple o miles up the estate road, savin wir feet.'

Once I had mollified the gamie on the phone and got permission to proceed beyond Invercauld gates, Mafia enthusiasm for the trip seemed to increase dramatically. I picked them up, full of high spirits, in the Lada, and endured the usual gamut of Lada-jokes with gritted teeth. They would eat their words, I swore, as we headed northwards.

In the teeth of forecasts of gales, sleet and even thunder we had decided to venture to the Howff in mid-winter. But the forecast was wrong. Instead the temperature fell and fell in the clear stillness, and the substantial snow-covering on the ground began to turn hard, and in places to sheet-ice. The heavily-laden Lada roared effortlessly over the De'il's Elbae, revelling in the challenge of a Siberian climate.

'A miracle o low-temperature physics, this machine,' I exulted as we stopped in Braemar for food and drink. But it was cold, and it was a long way to the Howff, we thought, as we ate and drank in the Fife, and I'm sure Erchie had an ulterior motive for telling me that there was a ceilidh on that night in the hotel, and the Dominie for mentioning that the establishment did a reasonably priced B&B...

'And then, we don't know this wreck of yours will get up the estate road,' the latter deprecated. But I refused to rise to this macho baiting, and walked instead to the door. And I did reflect that a man who drove around in the kind of thing Supermodels advertised should be careful of his words. I said nothing, and would do my talking on the road.

In a few minutes we were at the back road to Invercauld. I looked around for someone to tell we had permission to drive on it, found no-one and just headed up the glen. The ground was hard, but the frozen sand and the heaps of pine needles gave good grip, except for the occasional iced-over puddle. I kept a steady pace in low gear, and a firm grip on the wheel. We came to the gate where I had expected to leave the vehicle—but it was open.

'Jist drive on,' cries Erchie, 'they'll be lettin us go the hale distance tae the forest.' I was through before I had the chance to wonder whether he would have been so daring with the Boomerbus. But he was working on my psychology, praising the vehicle, comparing its handling favourably with the Boomerbus, admiring my driving skills as we moved along a track now little more than sheet ice, with a big drop down on our left. So, flattered—and noticing the Dominie was doing the silent white knuckled bit—I carried on another mile or so. Then, in drifts, we halted. We were there and I cast the Supermodel driver a withering look. But still he wouldn't let go.

'It probably won't start when we get back,' he ventured. I ignored that and began officiating at the distribution of the wood and tools, as we happit up.

Soon we were loaded and ready to go, dragging our wooden burdens behind us, forming a procession like Christ and the Thieves on their way to a wintry Golgotha. But we walked in beauty and delight. It was cold, how cold, snow scrunching on the path and ice crackling on the burns we crossed. But the hills were contoured in unbroken white, visible as in day beneath a sky holding a full moon and a million stars. We made good time until we got to the defile leading to the Howff. This had filled with drifting snow, through which a fair trail of footsteps had been broken. But heavily burdened, we floundered waist deep in the drifts, dragging our self-imposed crosses behind us, and cursing, sweating as we went. We followed the footsteps till I noticed.

'They've gone too far. They've missed it, look, they've turned roond and gaed back.'

The Dominie looked at the spoor and read the clear message. Two people, looking for the Howff before us, had not found it. We would worry about that later.

'It's up there,' I pointed.

And we dragged our planks, doubling as enormous ice-axes, over an inclined rising slope, to come at the Howff from behind. Round it stretched an unbroken membrane of purest, sparkling snow. It was ours, it had waited for us and our rituals. We entered, with reverence, and dumped our wood, laid out our belongings, hung up our food and masked a brew of tea. Sitting supping our brew, Erchie mentioned something I had already noticed.

'The door's been fixed. It fits perfectly.'

I decided I would worry about that 'the morn'—and then too, I might give a thought to what had happened to our unsuccessful precursors in the snow. They would have a cold night. The walls of the Howff, I noticed, were hung with ice about two inches thick—inside. I was warm in my double sleeping bag and on my thermal mattress. I hoped, as I put out the light, the lost duo were too. More we could not do for them.

We had expected, based on the Dominie's Iron Laws of Scottish Weather, that on the Hogmanay a warm front would have moved in. He had repeatedly informed us that you never get two consecutive good days of weather in Scotland in winter, for some scientific reason I forget. But if anything the day was better than its predecessor: a dazzling clear blue sky formed a hemisphere over the white, unbroken ground stretching to Beinn a' Bhuird. It was still, in air so cold it caught your breath. It was too good a day to spoil by puncturing my friend's meteorological mythology, so instead we breakfasted outside, and debated the day's plans. Firstly, the wood.

It was good wood, expensive, and I rejected the suggestion of a Hogmanay Bonfire with it—but there was no way I was carrying it back either. Facetious comments about installing a sauna or a corner bar I just ignored. And then I had it. A Seat. The Stobcross G.M.C. Memorial Bench, donated to the Howff—just the thing it needed. We set to it with a will. Erchie officiated, offering advice, cups of tea and wee nips as the Dominie and I measured, hammered and sawed. It was a fine way of keeping warm, as the temperature was still below zero, and we enjoyed our lunch in comfort, seated with our legs stretched out.

The Boomer and his lamp, the Dominie, and the Stobcross G.M.C. Memorial Bench

Physical creativity had stimulated other aspects of my Renaissance personality, and I felt inclined to honour the occasion with a poem. It came in a flash, and was soon in the bothy book.

Jesus wis a jiner
And Reverend Robertson tae
Bit me and Pete
Biggit the seat
Yer airse is on the day.

Erchie ventured that nobody would understand 'a' yon Aberdonian', but that was the point. Make it difficult for people, just like finding the Howff itself. A perusal of the book showed a little increase in usage over the decade, but still averaging only a couple of overnights a week, with virtually none in winter. Some entries expressed delight in having found it by their unaided efforts, unlike the duo whose steps we had seen last night...

'We should really go oot and look for yon lads,' I suggested, once we had tidied up after our work.

Now the Monklands Mafia have 'come out' as aspirant Corbetteers, and guilt by association has led certain snide elements to dub us The Three Corbetteers when I go away with them. So nothing minor like the possibility of a couple of corpses was going to prevent them getting above the 762 metre line. Opposite was Carn na Drochaide, an eminence so insignificant I had never noticed it on my countless previous visits to Slugain. Erchie suggested,

'Aye, we could follow the steps as far as the ruins o Slugain Lodge, and then maybe tak a wee daunder up Carn na Drochaide.'

As it transpired, conscience was salved and Corbett bagged. We had only gone a little distance through the floundering snow, when the errant pair popped up, emerging from one of the 'imitation' howffs near Slugain, where they had spent a roofless night. We conversed, discovering that they had indeed failed to find the doss, and spent a cold night in the open, luckily without encountering any precipitation. But they were miserable, and were calling it a day. They headed downglen, while we chested our way through the snow slopes to gain the rising plateau of our dubious eminence.

As often, experience surpassed expectation. As we rose, more and more came into view. The deepest green of the pines of the Quoich, stippled against the snow, itself ribboned by the blue of the river, lay below us, while behind Beinn a' Bhuird the whole of the 'Gorms came into view, Cairn Toul looking particularly fine far off. A circular walk round the summit cairn brought into view the lands of the Aberdeen-shire Gael, now an extinct species—the likes of Maggie Gruer are no more. On the way down I alternated the view of the Quoich pines with looking at the snow. A variety of animal tracks and scratchings covered it: fox, hare, deer. And in places where it was unbroken, the wind had etched a herring-bone weave on its surface. It was darkening ere we regained the Howff, to await The Bells.

Now, I had assured my companions that the Howff was a cosy place in winter. It was small, and warmed up easily, I insisted, and we would soon have those icicles off the walls, and take in the New Year in fine style. The plan was that, after eating, we would leave on the Primuses, and in addition we would have Diogenes' Lamp as well—that is, Erchie's turbo-charged Tilly lamp—to add to the heat. That was the plan. But the wind had scoured the snow off the tin roof of the Howff, and its normal winter igloo-qualities were lost. The stoves roared, the Tilly hissed, but the de'il of difference did it make. There was not even a drop of melt from the boots we had brought back into the Howff, not even a glaze of water on the icicles and sheet-ice which clad the walls. We were soon sitting on the bench in our sleeping bags, passing nips of cold whisky along with frozen hands, wishing midnight would come. It was a slow train coming.

Finally a trio of watches announced it was somewhere near midnight, five minutes either way. Erchie suggested to me,

'You are the first-footer. Oot ye go, see if ye can hear bells or somethin, and come back in if ye are sure it's next year.'

I was reluctant, but once outside found it was no colder, and the starlit heavens made it much more pleasant. I heard no bells, but, when it was safely another year, came in to wish my companions all the best. Despite the doss wanting a lum, I wished that any belonging to the Mafia would reek, and handed over my coal.

We observed the rituals. We had a hearty Auld Lang Syne despite the constrictions of the Howff, then passed round the Black Bun and the Water of Life. Sudden animation seemed to produce warmth, and we partied into the wee sma oors before bedding to a couple of lullabies from Erchie.

New Year's day was again splendid, and as we walked down the glen, with a snow-girt Lochnagar ahead of us, I could not help (despite the generally pervading feeling of goodwill) remarking to Pete that, unless I was mistaken, we had had three good winter days in a row. Though he has possibly not heard of it, the Dominie is a fervent believer in Quine's Law, which says that there is no theory, however absurd, that cannot be defended indefinitely by ad hoc supplementary hypotheses. The sum of his supplementary wisdom appeared to be that there is never more than one good day in winter, unless there are two or three, or even more.

Back at the car we found another vehicle. A massive macho-mobile, host to a trio of guys who had spent the past couple of days snow-holing on Beinn a' Bhuird and attempting the Crofton-Cumming, which had proved too thin. That, as we soon discovered, was to be the least of their worries.

The Lada started first time. No need for me to invoke Quine's Hypothesis here to explain a failure of predictions, I thought, as we drove back to the gate. A very locked gate. We pondered. Reverse the Lada through it. Take it off its hinges. Then Erchie did a few rough hand measurements.

'The wee pedestrian gate at the side, wi the cattle grid. It'll jist go through there, if ye gie a good run at it and pull the wheel roond when ye are aboot half wye through. But tak a good run at it.'

Despite wondering if he would have risked such cavalier treatment with the Boomerbus, there was nothing for it. With the Mafia watching—smirking I thought—I pointed the vehicle at the side gate and pushed down the accelerator. When the rummle of the grid was felt, I yarked the wheel to avoid a banking section, and pressed the pedal further. There was a batter as my side-mirrors folded inwards, but the vehicle soon stood proudly on the road again. Once more, Erchie gave credit where due, and announced the Boomerbus could not have performed the miracle just witnessed.

'Neither', observed the Dominie, 'will the one those three lads back the road are driving. They've got a problem.'

Whether, how, they resolved it we did not wait to see, but headed home. We had snatched a splendid trip from nothing, in a situation where obstacles seemed to fall away. And we had kept up, to no possible avail, some tradition. I still have the hinges and the sneck, they may yet come in useful. And the Lada.

Echo:
The Death of Deeside Gaelic

> The highlanders and people of the islands are a savage and untamed nation, rude and independent, given to rapine and easy living, comely in person yet unsightly in dress, hostile to the English people and language and exceedingly cruel.

So wrote John of Fordun, the Aberdeen chronicler, in 1380. And when he wrote, the 'Gaelic frontier' was only about thirty miles west of Aberdeen itself, and the language was spoken in half of Scotland. (By English, Fordun means Lowland Scots, then known as 'Inglis', i.e. language of the Angles. Gaelic he calls Scots, i.e. the language of the Scots from Ireland. Confusing possibly…but logical!)

Today even the optimists could hardly deny that—barring a few toeholds on the mainland—the frontier of the Gaidhealtachd is the water that separates the Hebrides from the rest of Scotland. Yet only half a century ago there were old people whose domestic tongue was Gaelic, living in the small village of Inverey just west of Braemar, in which itself Gaelic had been the everyday language till around 1900. Upper Deeside was the gradually retreating linguistic frontier between Gaelic and Lowland Scots for about six hundred years. The political influence of the Gaidhealtachd was ended with the defeat of the Jacobites, but had been in decline since the victory of the Aberdeen militia and their allies over MacDonald, Lord of the Isles, at the Battle of Harlaw in 1411. But the language survived another half millenium in upper Deeside: on the 'Braes o' Mar'. The area was recognised as hostile by lowland north-east folk who suffered the depredations of its caterans. One of the greatest north east ballads, ironically entitled 'Inverey' denounces its inhabitants as 'Vile Heilanmen, stealin oor kye (cattle)'. And this hostility translated into enthusiastic support for the Hanoverian troops of Cumberland when they came to Aberdeen in 1746, en route to Culloden.

Gradually upper Deeside was 'pacified' and the clan system broken up, and by the middle of the nineteenth century or so, upper Deeside was economically like many west Highland areas, with a crofting central belt, and a hinterland given over to sporting estates. Around 1900 it is clear that Gaelic was still flourishing, though no longer as the sole language it had been at the time of the Jacobite Rebellions in the eighteenth century. Then virtually none of the prisoners taken could speak anything but Gaelic. The fact that Lowland Scots soon penetrated the area is shown by an anecdote concerning the oldest surviving Jacobite, Peter Grant, known as the 'Dubrach'. In 1822, when he was 108, he was offered a pension by George IV, who called him 'his oldest friend'. The Dubrach replied, 'Na, na, I'm nae yer auldest freen, I'm yer auldest enemy'—but he took the pension! The ruins of the Dubrach's croft can be seen near the Chest o Dee. By about 1900 it seems that the ability to speak both Gaelic and Lowland Scots (Doric) was the norm, in a population of about 500 in Braemar and its surrounding region. Gaelic was still the main domestic language, and could be heard widely in the streets of Braemar as well.

The more mountainous areas around Braemar were cleared to make sporting estates: forty families were cleared from Glen Ey in the 1840s for example. But from the families of gamekeepers, children with no English were still coming to school in Inverey around the turn of the century. All of the gamekeepers who guarded the famous Corrour Bothy in the Lairig Ghru had Gaelic as their first tongue. Inverey itself was formed largely from those cleared from surrounding glens, and in 1881 about 85 of its population of 100 had Gaelic as their first language.

Inverey however, declined rapidly from a population of about 140 in 1841, to roughly 20 at the outbreak of World War II. Since crofting existed only in the south-west corner of Aberdeenshire, the county was excluded from the Crofters' Act of 1886, and tenants had no legal protection. It is difficult to avoid the conclusion that population loss caused by lack of economic opportunity was the main reason for the decline of Gaelic. Though the population did grow in Braemar itself, this was mainly due to economically active lowland north-easterners moving into the village, 'ferm lads, so ye aye got the Doric comin in, a lot o them settled in Braemar and they kent naethin of Gaelic' as one old man put it.

For those who blame anglicisation, by means of the Kirk and education, for Gaelic's decline, there is little evidence from Upper Deeside. Local presbyteries favoured Gaelic speakers, rejecting as minister in Braemar an English speaker for a Gaelic speaker in 1795. And while it is true that at the time of the Jacobite rebellions schools of the Society for the Propagation of Christian Knowledge favoured 'the more speedy extirpation of the Irish language', this policy was reversed, and in the nineteenth century schools were effectively bilingual, with the SPCK producing Gaelic dictionaries, catechisms and bibles. The main impact of education was to speed up emigration. As the Statistical Account said of upper Deeside, those who learned English 'immediately enter as clerks to commercial companies in different corners of the world'. It seems that poverty and educational opportunity, rather than repression, winnowed out the Gaelic from upper Deeside.

The supreme example of this was John Lamont, who attended school at Inverey. In 1817 he moved to a Scottish seminary in Ratisbon, and eventually became Johann von Lamont, Astronomer Royal of Bavaria. There is a monument to him in Inverey, with an inscription in English, German and Gaelic. But another interesting example is given by Queen Victoria in her *Highland Journal*. She talks of Prince Albert's Jäger (ghillie) 'who speaks (Gaelic) with great purity' giving him lessons and explaining place names, and mentions that the Jäger's son became an Attaché in Japan. On Deeside as elsewhere, education proved a double-edged sword for the Gael.

And if enthusiasm for culture was the answer, Gaelic would have survived in Deeside long after it did: once Victoria arrived, the language, Highland dress and Highland sports became very chic and received her patronage—but the decline continued. After 1914 it appears that Gaelic had become largely 'domesticated' in the Braes o' Mar, i.e. spoken in the home but not outside. Psycho-linguists suggest this is the last stage before irreversible decline.

In Inverey and Braemar the Gaelic was not supplanted by English, but by the very strong north-east version of Lowland Scots, Doric. This was not spoken by ministers or teachers, but by the economic incomers, or by those amongst whom the emigrants moved to work in Lowland Aberdeenshire, often on a temporary basis. Maggie Gruer is an example. Gaelic was her first language, but after World War I, no one is on record as hearing her talk anything but Doric. When she died in 1939, only a handful of people in Inverey had Gaelic. The last native speaker was a Mrs Bain, many of whose Gaelic sayings and stories were recorded by Adam Watson in the later 1970s. One of them serves as an interesting example of her bilingualism:

> Cha robh riamh gobhainn nach robh paiteach, cha robh riamh sagart nach robh sanntach.
> There wis nivver a smith that wisna thirsty, there wis nivver a priest that wisna greedy.

A historical irony for you: upper Deeside was once Gaelic speaking and Jacobite, now it is one of the strongest Doric speaking areas—and fervently Hanoverian! And the language of the Garden of Eden, in its last surviving pocket east of the Grampian mountains, where it had been spoken for a thousand years, is beyond resurrection.

But though all that meets your eyes, on Deeside or elsewhere, may be a dumb wall or a mute lazy-bed, you can still hear—if you listen carefully between the sounds of your own footfalls—the silent echo of those who were here before you, and whose heritors you are.